BREAKING PROMISES

DELTA FORCE STRONG
BOOK NINE

ELLE JAMES

TWISTED PAGE INC

Dedicated to my editor Delilah Devlin for keeping me in commas and polishing my story. She's also my awesome sister! Love her so much!

Elle James

AUTHOR'S NOTE

Enjoy other military books by Elle James

Delta Force Strong
Ivy's Delta (Delta Force 3 Crossover)
Breaking Silence (#1)
Breaking Rules (#2)
Breaking Away (#3)
Breaking Free (#4)
Breaking Hearts (#5)
Breaking Ties (#6)
Breaking Point (#7)
Breaking Dawn (#8)
Breaking Promises (#9)

Visit ellejames.com for titles and release dates
For hot cowboys, visit her alter ego Myla Jackson
at mylajackson.com
and join Elle James's Newsletter at
https://ellejames.com/contact/

BREAKING PROMISES

DELTA FORCE STRONG BOOK #9

New York Times & USA Today
Bestselling Author

ELLE JAMES

c

CHAPTER 1

"KETCH AND GONZO, IN POSITION." Xavier Gonzalez said into the radio. "Go!"

Asher "Smoke" Gray passed his two Delta Force teammates and leaped forward from one building to the next, the steady sound of rocket fire leading him toward his target. His Israeli Special Forces counterpart, David Nassar, kept pace with him, three steps behind. The two highly trained operators had chosen to take point as the most skilled snipers. Their mission was to take out the Hamas terrorists orchestrating the rocket bombardment of Israel that had gone on for the past three nights as retribution for the confiscation of a cargo ship carrying medical supplies destined for the Gaza Strip.

Israeli intelligence had received information that the ship had in fact contained medical supplies. However, buried beneath the medical supplies had been a massive shipment of arms to resupply Hamas on the Strip. The Israeli Navy intercepted the ship and took it into their base at the Port of Haifa.

As Smoke moved along the street, he clung to the shadows, careful not to expose himself to streetlights or potential sentries guarding the rocket launcher location. Once Smoke and Nassar were in position, Gonzo and Master Sergeant Karl Ketchum would follow. Voodoo, Rome, Ice and five men from the Israeli Special Forces, or Sayeret, had fanned out, moving forward on parallel streets, closing in on the target. If needed, they would provide a distraction to allow Smoke and Nassar to get close enough to take out their targets. Once they eliminated the men launching the rockets, they could work on disabling the rocket launcher. Blowing up the launcher wasn't an option, not when Hamas had parked it in the middle of a populated area. Destroying the launcher might ignite the remaining rockets and devastate the area. The civilian collateral damage wouldn't go unnoticed. Not with Hamas's news and social media propaganda machine.

Smoke peeked around the corner of a building toward an open area that appeared to have been a park. A truck with a hydraulic lift on the back stood in the park's center.

The launcher was nearly empty with only two rockets remaining. An additional stack of another six rockets stood several yards from the truck. Intel estimated Hamas had a stash of thousands of rockets to refill the battery and continue its onslaught. Destroying the launcher was imperative.

A group of men, armed with AK-47s, surrounded the truck and the launcher. Some guarded the perimeter. Others stared at the launcher.

With a quick, thorough assessment of the people standing in the park, Smoke raised his rifle and stared through his digital night vision scope, sighted in on the man wearing loose, black trousers and a black tunic, sporting an equally black turban on his head. He appeared to be the one in charge. The terrorist stood with his shoulders back, his head held high. A man approached him, carrying a radio on his back. He spoke briefly, nodded and turned away.

Smoke studied the leader who had a short, dark beard, high cheekbones, heavy eyebrows and a prominent nose. He matched the image of the Hamas leader they had been briefed on prior to executing this mission. He had the nose, the eyebrows and the high cheekbones, but he didn't have the scar from the corner of his right eye to the edge of his mouth, and his beard was shorter and darker. He waved his hand, and another rocket shot into the air with a fiery blast, shaking the ground around them. Only one rocket remained in the battery of empty shells.

Out of the corner of his eye, he saw Nassar moving into his position on the opposite side of the street, using the corner of another building as cover. Smoke waited until the other sniper had his rifle braced against his shoulder.

"I have the primary target in my sights." Smoke said softly into his mic, his finger resting lightly on the trigger.

"In position," Nassar said. "Secondary target acquired."

"Let's get this party started," Gonzo said. "Make it quick. We don't want to be surprised by incoming from the rear."

Smoke focused on his bogey. "Ready?" he whispered into his mic.

"Ready," Nassar responded.

"Ready," Ketch echoed.

"On three," Smoke said. "One...Two...Three." He held his breath and caressed the trigger. The silencer at the end of his barrel muffled the sound of the bullet leaving the rifle.

The leader's eyes widened. He stood still for a moment, and then fell to his knees and crashed to the ground. Another man near the launcher dropped at the same time.

At first, the other men around the park didn't

realize what was happening, giving Smoke and Nassar a chance to pick off two more each. By that time, shouts sounded, and the perimeter guards fired their AK-47s indiscriminately at the dark streets and alleys surrounding them.

The other Deltas and Israelis joined in the fight.

One of the Hamas men dropped to his belly, rolled behind the stack of rockets and fired toward the corners where Smoke and Nassar had established their positions.

Smoke couldn't return fire for fear of hitting the rockets and setting off a firestorm of explosions.

Instead, he had to withdraw behind the corner enough to protect himself and focus his attention on other men in less precarious and more exposed positions.

A moment later, a small dark object sailed through the air, landing in front of Nassar's face where he lay prone. He scrambled to his feet and kicked the object like a professional soccer player, aiming for a mid-field goal.

"Take cover!" he yelled and dove behind the building.

Smoke flung himself back behind the building, hoping the other joint team members did the same.

A blast sounded.

Smoke scrambled to his feet and ran, covering his ears.

A moment later, a deafening explosion ripped

through the sky, slamming through the surrounding structures. The force of the blast flung Smoke forward. He landed hard on his belly as debris erupted from buildings, raining down on him. He covered his head and the back of his neck with his arms and tucked his face into his shirt. The wall of the business beside him crumbled and toppled down, the bulk of which narrowly missed crushing him. Dust filled the air like a dense fog, making it impossible to see more than a foot in front of his face.

As soon as he could, Smoke lurched to his feet, his ears ringing and his lungs choking on the fine particles of dust filling the air. He pulled a large dark scrap of cloth from one of his cargo pockets and wrapped it around his face and neck, pulling it up over his mouth and nose to prevent the dust from entering his lungs. He tapped the headset on his helmet. "Deltas?"

A moment passed. Then another.

Silence.

His heart hammering against his ribs, Smoke turned in the eerie haze. Buildings around him were so damaged by the blast their walls were ruptured or gone. The street filled with rubble made it difficult to know what was street and what was building. Smoke didn't know where to begin looking for his teammates.

A man appeared out of the mist, his body

covered in a layer of gray, fine powder, a rifle in his hands.

Smoke raised his weapon, pointing at the man's chest. "Halt, who goes there?"

The man coughed. "Nassar," he choked out.

Smoke lowered his rifle and touched a finger to the side of his helmet. "Do you have coms?"

Nassar shook his head.

"We need to move to our extraction point," Smoke said through the cloth over his face.

"The others?" Nassar coughed and covered his mouth with the front of his shirt as he dragged in a shaky breath.

"The others will move toward the extraction point. We'll regroup there." And count heads. If anyone was missing, Smoke would be back to find him.

Nassar nodded and started down the middle of the street, his rifle held ready to fire.

Smoke followed, turning around every so often to check his six. As he passed another crumbled building, the pile of rubble near his feet stirred.

Smoke jumped back, aiming his weapon at the debris.

A figure emerged and staggered to his feet. He carried a dirty rifle and wore a helmet covered in the thick powder caused by the destruction.

Smoke leaned toward him. "Ketch?"

"Yeah," the man responded and hacked up half his lung. "Where's Gonzo?"

A couple of yards away, what had appeared to be debris from a fallen wall, rolled over. "Here," Gonzo called out, raising a hand as if at roll call in school. "Did you get the number of the truck that hit me?"

Smoke hurried over to him, extended a hand and hesitated. "Injuries?"

"My ears are ringing so loud I can't think, and my head hurts like a mother fuc—" He curled into a ball and coughed hard. One hand clutched at his belly, the other at his head, and he moaned.

His own head aching from the force of the concussion, Smoke understood. "We need to get moving before reinforcements pour in and cut us off from our extraction point."

Gonzo gripped Smoke's hand.

As Smoke braced himself, the other man pulled himself to his feet, standing a few inches shorter than Smoke. He swayed for a second, then squared his shoulders, a frown pulling his brow low. "Hear anything from the others?"

Smoke tapped the side of his helmet and shook his head. "My comms are out."

"Mine, too," Ketch said.

"Same," Gonzo added. "Hopefully, the others are on their way."

They moved quickly through the streets, back to the water where the combat rubber raiding rafts had been stashed between the myriad of fishing boats in the Port of Gaza, waiting to take them out under cover of darkness as they arrived. They could have beached the Zodiac watercraft on the long stretch of beach, but they'd determined it would be easier to hide among the fishing and pleasure boats moored near the port. And it was easier to find cover and concealment there than on an empty beach in the open.

Smoke took the lead, his hearing still impacted but slowly improving. They had a lot of ground to cover in a short amount of time.

Sirens sounded, moving toward them.

Smoke ducked into a dark alley. Gonzo, Ketch and Nassar followed.

An ambulance raced past them, heading for ground zero of the rocket explosion.

"I only heard the grenade and then one rocket go off. From what I could see, there was a stack of six more rockets lying on the ground," he said.

"We're lucky they didn't all explode," Gonzo said.

"We wouldn't be walking here if they had," Ketch said, his jaw set in a tight line.

"Hopefully, the one rocket destroyed the launcher, so they can't load the remaining six," Smoke said.

After the ambulance passed, Gonzo took a step toward the street.

Smoke snagged his arm and pulled him back.

A truck raced past moments later, filled with heavily armed Hamas soldiers, hurrying to get to the site of the explosion.

"Thanks," Gonzo said.

Smoke hoped all the team had gotten out. The terrorists wouldn't go easy on any opposing forces found deep inside enemy territory.

They continued through the streets, avoiding any other humans at all costs. They weren't supposed to be behind the enemy lines. And the US Delta Force operatives weren't supposed to get involved with the ongoing war between the Palestinians and the Israelis.

Then why the hell was Delta Force in Gaza? And why were they helping the Israeli Defense Force Sayerets curb the delivery of rockets that were lobbed into villages of innocent Israeli civilians? The politicians in Washington must have decided to provide assistance as a show of benevolence and support of the Israeli government. The Deltas were mere pawns in their global political wargames.

Smoke had a lot of respect for the men and women of the Sayarets, having been on another mission recently into the West Bank. They were a highly-trained unit of fierce fighters, every bit as good as what the US had to offer. He was proud to work alongside them. The death and destruction Hamas served up daily needed to stop. Until it did, there would be no negotiations between the two sides.

Ahead, Smoke caught glimpses of the starlight reflecting off the water of the Mediterranean Sea. His pulse quickened along with his footsteps. Movement in his peripheral vision made him look to his right as he crossed a street.

A dark figure, carrying a heavy load on his back, moved from shadow to shadow, heading toward the sea on a street parallel to the one on which Smoke currently stood.

Smoke raised his fist, indicating the others should halt. He ran down the cross street and slipped up behind the man, carrying his load.

The burden he carried moaned and moved an arm.

He wasn't dead. But, depending on his injuries, he could go south quickly.

When Smoke was within ten feet of the man, he called out softly, "Marco," he challenged.

"Polo," the man responded.

Though the face was completely covered in dust, relief flooded Smoke as he recognized the voice. "Voodoo," he said. "Who's this?"

"Rome," he answered, his tone terse. "The blast knocked him backward. He hit the ground hard. He also caught some shrapnel. It's embedded in his left shin."

Moving back into the shadows, Smoke took one of Rome's arms and moved in closer. "I'll take him."

Voodoo, legally known as Beau Guidry, shook his head. "I've got him."

"Dude, you brought him far enough." Smoke handing his weapon to Gonzo. "Let me take over."

Ketch and Gonzo lifted Rome off Voodoo's shoulder and settled him onto Smoke, piggy-back style.

"Hold on, buddy. We'll get you back." With his arms looped around Rome's legs, Smoke took off, heading for the port.

Ketch and Gonzo took point. Voodoo and Nassar had Smoke's six. They moved quickly. Smoke hoped that the other members of their team would be waiting at the dock, already in the boats, ready to punch out.

Ahead, Ketch raised his fist.

Smoke stopped, clinging to the shadow of a building. Rome's breath on the back of his neck reassured him that the man was still alive.

Ketch gave the signal to follow him, and they continued through the streets.

A block short of the port, they stopped in an alley between buildings.

"I'm going forward," Ketch said. "I'll flash a red light once if the boats are compromised. Twice for all clear." The man slipped away, moving quickly and silently past the buildings and across the road in front of the rudimentary Port of Gaza.

Voodoo and Nassar positioned themselves several yards to their rear, guarding their rear. Gonzo left Smoke's rifle leaning against the side of the building next to Smoke and Rome. He moved to the end of the block, knelt at the forward edge of the building there and covered for Ketch while he made his way to the boats.

Smoke leaned his back, with Rome, against a building and waited for what seemed like forever. "Hanging in there, Rome?" he asked.

Rome grunted.

"So, you're still with us, huh?" Smoke nodded. "Don't worry. We'll get you back to Jerusalem before you know it."

"Sure," Rome said, his voice weak.

"You know," Smoke said. "No man left behind."

"Damn right," Rome whispered.

A moment later, a pinpoint of red light flashed once amid the fishing boats tied to the pier.

Smoke tensed and leaned forward, taking all of Rome's weight. He held his breath, praying for the second flash for all clear.

After the longest second of his life, the red light flashed a second time.

Smoke released the breath he'd been holding and leaned forward, taking all of Rome's weight he'd been resting against the wall. "That's our cue. Let's blow this joint."

He waved to Voodoo and Nassar. When they were within a couple of yards of him, he turned toward the sea, quickly closing the distance between him and Gonzo.

Gonzo checked right and left then stepped out into the open. "Go," he said.

Smoke moved as quickly as he could with the man on his back across the open space, the street and onto the pier.

Once again, his team surrounded him, moving quickly. As they approached the location where they'd tucked the boats between a row of fishing boats, Ketch straightened from a kneeling position, and men rose from where they sat in the rubber crafts. They held out their arms for Rome.

Gonzo and Ketch eased the man off Smoke's back and handed him down into one of the boats. Voodoo and Gonzo dropped over the side of the pier into the same boat.

"Everyone here?" Smoke asked.

Ketch nodded. "All present. Get in. We've pushed our luck so far."

Smoke glanced behind him once more.

The dark silhouettes of men moving their way made his pulse quicken. "Time to bug out."

Ketch swore. "Couldn't wait another five minutes, could they?"

Smoke dove into the boat as the boat drivers fired up the engines. The first boat took off with its load of Sayerets and Deltas.

Ketch remained on the pier a moment longer than Smoke, his weapon trained on the approaching men. As soon as the engine roared to life, Ketch dropped down into the boat. As soon as his feet hit the rubber, the driver whipped the boat around and raced through the maze of fishing boats.

Shouts and shots rang out behind them.

Smoke, Gonzo, Nassar and others fired back as they broke free of the moored boats and headed out into open water.

For a moment, Smoke breathed a sigh of relief.

Then what appeared to be an old military-style PT boat whipped out of the port behind them, men on the front of the rig firing.

The military boat, made for moving swiftly through the water, would catch them before long.

Smoke conserved his ammunition until the larger, faster boat got closer. The Zodiac rubber boats bounced in the swells.

His heart pounding, Smoke held onto the boat and his weapon as the advancing boat closed the distance between them.

Just when Smoke raised his weapon to fire, the rapid staccato of fifty-caliber machinegun fire rent the air overhead.

Despite the rain of bullets, the trailing vessel didn't slow until a flash of light and an explosion ripped through the hull. The boat rocked to a stop, fire rising from the deck.

Without slowing, the Zodiacs continued out to sea a little further. The Chinook helicopter above made a wide circle, then lowered to the water, immersing its belly enough to lower the ramp. The first rubber boat sped up and drove up the ramp and into the chopper. Without hesitating, Smoke's boat driver followed, picking up speed. When the rubber hit the ramp, they slid up into the fuselage. Men leaped over the sides, grabbed the sides of the rubber raft and hauled it the rest of the way into the bird. The ramp rose as the helicopter lifted out of the water and into the sky.

They weren't safe until they were well beyond the range of heat-seeking missiles. The chopper rose high into the sky and headed north toward Tel Aviv. When they were far enough away, Smoke dared to breathe normally.

The team medic had Rome hooked up to an IV and had dressed his wound, stabilizing the man until they reached a higher level of medical care.

Smoke leaned back on the bench, his head pounding, his hearing barely returned to normal.

"Well, that didn't go quite as planned," Gonzo said.

Several helmets flew across the interior of the

helicopter at Gonzo, and some of the men chuckled, breaking the tension.

No, the operation hadn't gone as planned, but if Smoke had learned anything in his thirteen years in the military...plans were useless, but planning was necessary. What was done was done. They'd accomplished their mission. The rocket launcher had been destroyed.

Along with half a city block because a Hamas terrorist had thought it was a good idea to lob a grenade.

The mission debrief and after-action report would be interesting, to say the least. They might all be reassigned after what had happened.

CHAPTER 2

"DANNY, IS MY TIE STRAIGHT?" James Turner appeared in the doorway to Danica Turner's room inside the US Embassy in Jerusalem.

Danny smiled at her uncle. "I can't believe you still don't know how to tie a bow tie. How many years have you been in the state department?"

"Ties were always Ruth's job." Uncle James tugged at the listing bowtie. He dropped his hands to his sides. "She did it so well."

"She was the perfect partner, wasn't she?" Danny's heart squeezed as she crossed the room and pulled the bowtie loose. "You miss her."

"Terribly," her uncle said with a crooked, sad smile. "I'm glad you decided to join me for a few months. I feel so lost without her."

"It was Dad's idea, but I'm glad he suggested it," Danny admitted. "I'd had my fill of the MMA ring."

She made quick work of the bowtie, finishing with a wave of her hand. "There. Almost as good as Aunt Ruth's work."

Her uncle hugged her and stepped back. "I don't know how a lovely young woman could participate in such a violent sport as mixed martial arts."

"Maybe I needed a place where I could work out my anger issues after leaving active duty." She shrugged. "It doesn't matter. I'm done with that chapter of my life. Now, I just need to figure out what I want to do next. Being here, with you, gives me a chance to decide what my next chapter will be." She smiled up at her uncle, a man who looked so much like her father, the man who'd set the bar for all men in her life, which was both good and bad. At thirty years old, she'd thought she'd have a partner, lover or husband by now. Not one man she'd dated had come even close to that bar. And what man wanted a woman who could take him down in the blink of an eye? Most men wanted delicate, helpless women who appealed to their protector gene.

"I appreciate that you're here," her uncle said. "You have no idea how much."

"As much as I appreciate the opportunity, I'm sure." She stood back. "Now, let's go down to dinner before everyone starves to death." Her own stomach rumbled noisily.

Her uncle laughed. "Namely you?"

Her cheeks heated. "Yes. I used to eat a lot of calories to maintain muscle mass and my crazy workout schedule." She still worked out to stay strong, just not as many hours each day.

"By all means. Let's feed this woman before she arm-wrestles me for breadcrumbs." He smiled at her, his gaze skimming her length. "By the way, you look beautiful in that dress."

Danny tugged at the thin straps to the sapphire-blue dress that hugged her body like a second skin, dipping so low in the back, she was afraid she'd offend someone with its suggestiveness. "Are you sure it's not too risqué?"

"Not at all. You're a young woman with a pretty figure. Why not show it off?"

Some of her costumes in the MMA competitions had been just as skimpy. Only they'd made her feel more badass than delicate. This dress made her feel…girlie. She hadn't felt that way since before her mother had died when she was only eleven years old. Her father had taken over raising her from there, introducing her to all the things he loved doing. She'd learned to hunt, fish, jog, workout and had become a black belt in taekwondo. When she'd graduated high school, she'd had no desire to continue her formal education by attending college and had chosen a military career instead, joining the Army at eighteen. Calling her a tomboy was an understatement. Thus, her discomfort wearing a beautiful long gown and high heels.

Her uncle held out his arm. "Shall we show off that dress?"

She nodded. After all, being the niece of the US Ambassador to Israel was like being in the MMA ring. Ninety-five percent of the time was spent looking like she belonged. The other five percent was proving she did.

So, the costumes were different. She felt no more comfortable in the dress than she had in the skimpy outfits she'd worn for the fights. Her sponsors had insisted on more skin, less material. Whether she wore a sports bra and bikini bottoms, or a dress cut down in the back to her butt crack, she was still the same, strong woman inside. If any man tried to hurt her or her uncle, she'd take him down.

Her family wanted her there to look out for her uncle, who'd received death threats since a medical supply ship destined for Gaza had been confiscated by the Israeli Navy. Hamas blamed the US government and the Israeli military equally since the US had promised to guarantee its safe passage to the port of Gaza.

Danny had only agreed to come after they assured her that James Turner needed a bodyguard. The idea of being a bodyguard had intrigued her enough to agree. And she loved her Uncle James and had loved her Aunt Ruth as well. Helping him through the threat and his grief had more meaning than pounding an opponent into the mat in the middle of a crowded arena.

Danny had burned through her anger over her time in the Army and had worked out some of her aggression from her military sexual trauma, or MST, as her Veterans Administration therapist termed it.

After leaving the Army, she'd vowed never to be vulnerable to a man's superior strength again. She'd worked hard to keep that promise to herself.

"Did you hear that we're getting a team of Delta Force Operatives here at the embassy?" her uncle asked as they descended the steps to the level where the dining room was located.

Danny frowned. "No, I didn't. When is that supposed to happen?" She wasn't sure she'd like having Army men running around the halls and grounds of the embassy. Her time in the Army hadn't been the best. Yeah, she'd made some life-long friends. But it had taken only one bad experience to shake her free of blind patriotism. She'd been raped and her career threatened by a sergeant in her chain of command. The man had nearly gotten away with it.

"I expect the Deltas anytime. I thought they would be here this evening, but they must've been delayed. They've been in Jerusalem conducting joint training with the Israeli Special Forces. One of their members was supposed to report to me as soon as they arrived." Her uncle stopped short of the dining room and glanced at his watch. "Shoot. I forgot the notes I made for my speech at dinner. I need to go to my office before I go into the dining room." He turned back toward the staircase; his office was on the first floor of the building.

Danny grabbed his arm, pulling him to a halt. "You need to go in and take your seat. Your staff is waiting for their dinner."

"But I need my notes."

"I'll get them," Danny said. "It won't take me a few minutes. Please start dinner without me."

"But you're the one who's so hungry," her uncle argued. "You go in and ask them to serve. I'll run to my office."

"Uncle," she said, shaking her head, "if I'm to be of assistance to you, you have to stop treating me like a guest and let me help."

He frowned for a moment, and then his lips turned up on the sides. "You're quite right, my dear. They'll wait until I return even if you tell them to go on without me." He patted her arm. "Thank you. The notes are on a typed sheet of paper in the middle of my desk. I don't know why I forgot them."

Danny smiled. "I'm sure someone came into

your office and distracted you. You're a busy man. You can't be expected to remember everything."

"I wouldn't be nearly as effective without my competent staff," he said.

"Your hungry, competent staff." Danny turned her uncle toward the dining room. "Go. I'll only be a few minutes."

After her uncle entered the dining room, Danny hurried for the stairs and descended to the first floor. Her feet clicked on the polished marble floor. Not used to wearing high heels, she kind of liked the tapping sound her shoes made and the way they showed off the definition of the muscles in her calves. She worked hard for those muscles and the strength she'd gained since her separation from the military.

At her uncle's office door, she paused. The door wasn't closed as it usually was. Instead, it stood slightly ajar, a soft light glowing within.

Her uncle often forgot to turn off the desk lamp before he left, but he always pulled the door shut.

A tingle of awareness rippled through Danny as she nudged the door wider and peered into the office with its dark mahogany desk, wood-paneled walls and floor-to-ceiling bookshelves.

As she'd suspected, the lamp glowed on the desk, and a white sheet of paper lay in the light.

Danny shook her head and pushed the door wider.

As she stepped forward, a movement in the corner of her eye caught her attention. A shadowy figure emerged from behind the door.

Reflexes kicked in, and Danny reacted to the imminent threat.

When a hand reached toward her, she grabbed it, yanked hard, ducked her shoulder and plowed into a tall, muscular man, flipping him over her shoulder.

He landed flat on his back, rolled to his feet and lunged for her.

Danny ducked to the side, dropped low and swept her high-heel-clad foot out, catching the man at the ankles.

He went down, landing on his belly. When he tried to push up, she snagged his left wrist out from under him and yanked his arm up behind his back and between his shoulder blades.

When he bucked and tried to get up, she straddled his hips and sat down on him. "Move, and I'll break your arm," she warned.

"Sweet Jesus, woman," he said. "Get off my back."

She pushed his arm further up the middle of his back. "Not until you tell me how you got past security and what you're doing in this office."

"Maybe you should tell me what *you're* doing in this office and how *you* got past security," he countered. "And I suggest you get off my back before I forcibly remove you."

She snorted. "Like you could." A tingling awareness ignited the nerves of her thighs and buttocks where they connected with the man's hips and tight ass. His broad shoulders indicated a man who took physical conditioning seriously. She almost hated hurting him. At the same time, she reveled in the fact she'd taken him down and kept him down.

"I could turn you over on your happy little ass in a heartbeat," he said. "But the moment you stepped through that door in that tight, sexy dress, I chose not to destroy your outfit. However, if you don't let me up soon…"

She leaned close to his ear. "Do I hear a threat?"

A low growl rumbled from his throat, causing a stir of excitement inside Danny.

"Try me," the man said.

Danny's muscles tensed in response to the challenge in his tone.

His muscles tensed beneath her.

It was about to be a rough ride. Danny was ready.

The overhead lights blinked on.

"Danny?" Uncle James's voice echoed against the wood-paneled walls. "What the hell?"

"I found this man lurking in your office," Danny said. "When he attacked me, I took him down."

"I wasn't attacking you," said the guy beneath

her. "I was reaching for the door when you pushed it open."

"Yeah?" she said. "And why were you opening the door? You shouldn't be in here after hours."

"Danny, honey," Uncle James said. "Let the man up."

"He could be a danger to you," she said, still sitting on the man and pushing his arm up the middle of his back. "He hasn't told us why he's here."

"There are less painful ways of obtaining that information," the man gritted out. "For both you and me."

"Danny." Her uncle used that same tone of voice her father used when he was getting stern with her. "Let the man get up off the floor. It's okay. He's not here to hurt me."

"Then why was he lurking in your office?" Danny refused to relinquish her hold on the intruder, half expecting him to come up fighting.

"Because I told the security staff that's where I wanted him to wait for me when he arrived." Her uncle touched a hand to her shoulder. "He's one of the team of Deltas just assigned to the embassy. He's here to help, not hurt."

She studied the man, dressed in civilian clothing. "But he's not wearing a uniform. Are you sure?"

"I can show you my military ID," he offered. "If you'll let me reach for my wallet."

Heat burned up Danny's neck into her cheeks. She let go of his hand and scrambled to her feet, smoothing her long dress over her hips and thighs.

The man pushed to his feet and turned piercing gray eyes on her, a smile tugging at the corners of his mouth. He reached into his pocket for his wallet. "I'm Sergeant Asher Gray, US Army," he said. "You must be the ambassador's niece." He pulled his military ID out of his wallet.

Danny frowned and nodded. "I am." She took the ID and studied it and him. Either it was a good fake or the man in front of her was indeed Sergeant Asher Gray, making Danny feel very stupid for taking him down while wearing a formal gown.

Her uncle chuckled and held out his hand in greeting. "Sergeant Gray, pleased to meet you."

Sergeant Gray gripped the ambassador's and gave it a firm shake. "The pleasure's mine."

Uncle James tipped his head toward Danny. "Please excuse my niece's enthusiasm for protecting me. I hope she didn't hurt you."

"No, sir. She didn't hurt me. I just didn't want to hurt her," the Delta said. "Sir, please, call me Smoke."

"Call sign?" Danny's uncle asked.

The broad-shouldered Delta nodded. "Yes, sir."

"Fitting." Her uncle released the man's hand. "This is my niece," he said. "Danica Turner."

The man called Smoke held out his hand to Danny.

Still hesitant and slightly embarrassed, Danny took his hand. As she did, he smiled, his eyes dancing with humor. A shock of electricity ripped up her arm and spread throughout her body. The man had black hair, graying slightly at the temples. Yet, his face was younger than the gray hairs intimated. He was so ruggedly handsome he took her breath away.

That had never happened to Danny. And she'd been around some gorgeous MMA fighters. None of them had looked like this man with his square jaw and quickly emerging five-o'clock shadow. His hand squeezed hers slightly, the warmth of his skin making heat build at her core. Shocked at the correlation, Danny yanked her hand out of his and hid it behind her back, sure it was shaking.

"Now that you two have met," her uncle said, "please, join us for dinner."

The man nodded. "It would be my pleasure. It's been a while since I've had something other than MREs."

"Then, you're in for a treat. Our chef is quite talented." He clapped a hand on Smoke's shoulder, and then passed him, lifted the paper off the desk, folded it into a small square and tucked it into his

31

pocket. "Have your men found quarters?" He started for the door.

Smoke walked with him. "Yes, sir," he said. "They're in the hotel across the street from the embassy. I understand one of us will be required to stay in the embassy." He reached for the door handle and held the door wide for the ambassador.

Danny followed behind her uncle. As she approached the Delta, she frowned.

"Sorry to disappoint you," Smoke said with a grin.

"Disappoint?" she asked, her frown deepening.

"I sense you were hoping I was an enemy combatant."

"I'm not disappointed. You were lurking in the dark, ready to pounce. I did what I was trained to do." She crossed the threshold then paused to meet his gaze. "I disabled the attacker."

"Fair enough." Smoke pulled the door closed behind him and rubbed his arm. "You've got some moves, Ms. Turner."

Her uncle laughed. "My niece has some special skills. She's not one to be messed with."

Smoke's mouth twisted. "A little late for the warning. And you're right. She has some mad skills."

Danny smirked. "Next time, don't wait in the dark. It smacks of burglar, mugger or terrorist."

He dipped his head; his lips curled into a crooked smile. "Point made, ma'am."

"And don't call me ma'am," she snapped, her brow dipping before it rose again. "You can call me Danny."

He nodded. "Danny, it is. And it's a pleasure to meet you."

She snorted softly. "I bet."

They followed Danny's uncle up the stairs and into the dining room, where he introduced Smoke to the members of his staff who resided in the embassy. Not every member of his staff lived inside the walls. Some preferred to live on the economy in apartments or townhomes and had left at the end of the workday to eat at their homes.

Still, the table was full of staff members patiently awaiting dinner.

The waitstaff hurried to place the food in front of each guest, and soon, they were all eating and talking among each other.

Danny sat to the right of her uncle.

Smoke sat directly across from her.

Once the meal had been consumed and the plates cleared to make way for dessert, her uncle cleared his throat. "Ladies and gentlemen, I received intelligence indicating a threat to all Americans in Israel. The Hamas faction operating in Gaza is blaming us for last night's explosion and the subsequent destruction of a medical facility, killing a doctor and several patients."

A barrage of questions followed from the staff, each member talking at once.

Uncle James raised his hand. "I don't know the specifics of how that came to pass or who was responsible, but the Palestinians and Hamas are pointing their fingers at the US and Israelis. That means, we need to keep on our toes for possible terrorist activities. There's also the possibility this embassy could become a target. We've been given additional support from the US Army, but you still need to practice situational awareness and bear with the tightened security. Thank you all for your support and continued sacrifices. We couldn't perform our diplomatic duties without all of you. Now, enjoy your dessert. I hear it's one of the chef's best." He started to sit, changed his mind, and smiled. "My apologies. Where are my manners as the host? Let me introduce Asher Gray," he waved his hand toward Smoke. His gaze shifted to Danny. "Asher is…my niece's fiancé. Please congratulate them and welcome Asher to the embassy."

Danny fought to keep the shock from her face and pasted on a smile as members of the staff congratulated her and Smoke on their "engagement."

"Show us the ring," one of the women called out.

Heat filled Danny's face, and she clutched her hands in her lap.

Smoke smiled and said, "It's at the jeweler's shop being fitted. I didn't get the right size." He pushed to his feet. "If you'll excuse me, I'd like to get settled in."

Danny laid her napkin on her plate. "Please, excuse me as well. My fiancé, my uncle and I have a lot to catch up on." She pinned her uncle with a steady stare.

The older man had taken his seat and spread his napkin on his lap. He sighed, laid his napkin on his plate and pushed to his feet. "Please excuse me. My niece is correct. We have a lot to catch up with her fiancé." He smiled and led the way from the room.

Smoke appeared at Danny's side, smiled down at her and offered her his arm.

She took it, forcing a smile to her tight lips, and followed her uncle from the room.

Once on the staircase leading up to her uncle's quarters, she muttered, "Fiancé? Really?"

"We'll discuss it in my quarters," Smoke said in clipped tones. "Not before."

Danny released her hold on Smoke's arm and followed her uncle up the stairs and through his apartment door.

Smoke kept pace, pulling the door closed behind them.

Once they were alone, Danny planted her hands

on her hips. "Would you care to explain what just happened?"

Her uncle faced her, a crooked smile forming on his lips. "Please, Danny. Play along. I didn't want to frighten the staff any more than my announcement could have. I had to come up with a cover story for Smoke without alerting my employees of the imminent threat. There have been direct threats against the US Ambassador to Israel. My boss sent the Deltas to protect me and my family... you." He drew in a deep breath. "He wants me to always have at least one Delta with me. As a bodyguard. Smoke is our guy. To do that without raising red flags, I needed a cover story. I'd been scrambling for one that would sound plausible. When I found you on the floor with Smoke, it came to me." He grinned and spread his arms wide. "An engagement."

"You could have clued us in before announcing it to the other members of the staff," Danny grumbled. "I'm sure my reaction wasn't all that convincing."

"You were fine," her uncle said. "And I didn't firm up the idea until after we'd returned to the dining room. It's the perfect cover for a bodyguard, for both you and me."

Anger burned inside Danny. "I thought I was acting as your bodyguard and assistant."

Her uncle nodded. "Of course, you are. Only, it will be even better with two bodyguards. Twice the coverage, and no one needs to know that other than the three of us."

"I don't know why you didn't want your staff to know," Danny said. "You trust them, don't you?"

"I do, but the fewer people who know, the more likely we'll keep it on the down-low. I don't want anyone outside these walls to know I'm worried. Hamas is getting more daring, striking targets inside the city of Jerusalem. Only yesterday, a shopping center was struck, and four people were critically injured."

Danny nodded. "I was in that market two days ago."

"You shouldn't go into crowded markets for a while," her uncle said. "I don't want you hurt by the terrorists."

She nodded. "I'll keep that in mind. But from here forward, I need to know all the intel, and your plans involving me, before you announce them to the world."

Her uncle nodded. "Fair enough." He faced Smoke. "You've said very little through all of this. Are you agreeable to my plan?"

With a smile, Smoke held open his arms. "I'm game. Should we seal the deal with a kiss?"

Danny's lips twisted. She turned and walked

toward the door, pausing with her hand on the doorknob. She snorted softly. "Sure. Seal the deal with a kiss. But you'll have to kiss my uncle. It's his deal."

CHAPTER 3

SMOKE LAUGHED as Danny left the room. He glanced back at her uncle.

Ambassador Turner shook his head, a smile pulling at his lips. "You two will need to come up with a plausible story to convince anyone who asks about your engagement." He pinned Smoke with his gaze. "Are you okay with this? It was the best I could do in the spur of the moment."

Smoke nodded, a frown pulling at his brow. "Your niece didn't appear happy about the charade."

Her uncle laughed. "She'll come around. Danny is one of the strongest women I know. Her only weakness I can see is her attitude toward men. She doesn't talk about it, but I suspect whatever caused it happened while she was on active duty in the Army. From what my brother said, she got out with a diagnosis of PTSD from what she saw and dealt with. I think it had more to do with friendly fire than enemy engagement."

Smoke's lips pressed together. All that he could think of was sexual harassment or abuse. "Too often, the good-ol'-boy system sweeps problems under the rug. A few men can make life horrific for the women serving in our military. Too often, nothing is done to stop it or punish those responsible."

Ambassador Turner's eyes narrowed. "You'll be responsible for protecting my niece and me. I'm counting on you being a good man."

Smoke raised a hand as if swearing an oath inside a courtroom. "Sir, I take my duties seriously. Your lives are mine to protect, not abuse. I'll do my very best."

The ambassador held his gaze a moment longer before finally nodding. "I consider myself a good judge of character. I believe you. Now, go speak to my niece and come up with a backstory to feed the people if you're asked about your engagement."

Smoke nodded. "Yes, sir."

"And Smoke…"

"Sir?"

"My niece doesn't take crap from anyone, least of all a man," the ambassador said.

A smile curved Smoke's lips as he rubbed the arm she'd twisted behind his back. "I gathered that in the first ten seconds with her."

Turner chuckled. "She's strong, fight-ready and capable. But I know the girl she was before the Army. She has a big heart and is very loyal to the people she loves. You two will be playing the part of an engaged couple. It will be easy to start to believe it's real." He pinned him again with a hard stare.

"Don't worry, sir. I know this is a role to play."

"I'm not worried about you remembering that," the ambassador said. "I'm more worried about Danny. Don't hurt her." He tipped his head to the left. "You can find her in the apartment next to mine. I have you assigned to the suite on the other side of hers. You'll need to be close if you're to be effective as a bodyguard."

"Yes, sir," Smoke said. He turned and left the ambassador, a frown pulling on his brow. That the ambassador thought he would hurt his niece had him shaking his head. He was on an assignment. The ambassador and his niece were part of that assignment. They were the job. Nothing more. He was responsible for their physical well-being. Falling in love with the niece wasn't part of the equation. Nor was her falling in love with him. He'd have to make sure she understood the rules going in.

Not that she seemed the type to fall in love easily.

His frown lifted as he recalled how quickly

she'd pinned him to the ground. All while wearing a dress and high heels. It would be interesting playing the part of a loving fiancé to a woman who could kick his ass. To keep that from happening again, he'd have to be on his toes at all times.

Her uncle didn't have to worry about anyone taking advantage of Danny. She could take care of herself. She'd mastered the skills to repel an unwelcome advance from a man.

Smoke wondered how she'd react to a welcome advance from a man. Would she pour all that energy and passion into her response? And what kind of man would have what it takes for her to welcome his attention? A very patient man, given what she'd probably experienced at the hands of some bastard in the military.

He stopped in front of her door and raised his hand to knock. Before his knuckles touched the wooden panel, the door was jerked open.

Danny grabbed his upraised hand and yanked him through the door.

As soon as he was across the threshold, she dropped his hand and shoved the door closed.

He braced himself, ready for her attack. She'd caught him off guard once. He couldn't let her best him twice. Smoke stood in a fighting position, his knees bent, hands raised, ready for Danny's next move.

She turned to face him, her brow furrowing. "Why are you standing that way?"

He shook his head. "Once bitten, twice shy," he said. "You surprised me before. I'm ready this time."

Danny rolled her eyes. "What do you think I'm going to do? Attack you?" She marched past him. "Now that I've established that you're not the enemy, I don't need to subdue you. Relax." Danny spun and planted her fists on her hips, looking like a Valkyrie ready for battle. "What are we going to do about this game my uncle has set us up to play?"

Smoke straightened yet kept his distance in case the woman decided he was a threat after all. "We play along," he said. "Your uncle doesn't want to appear too concerned and scare the rest of his staff. You and I can provide the protection he needs without drawing too much attention to him or the situation."

"I was doing that anyway, without the added burden of a fiancé," she said. "I don't know why he didn't just let you and your team appear to supplement the grounds security and let me do what I came here to do."

Smoke's eyes narrowed. "You came here to provide protection for your uncle?"

Danny nodded. "Yes, I did. My family thought he needed more than what the US government provides and asked me to fly out to help. I quit my gig in the MMA arena to do this for my uncle."

"MMA?" Smoke frowned.

"Mixed Martial Arts."

His eyes widened. "You were an MMA fighter?"

She nodded. "For three years."

Smoke ran a hand through his hair. "No wonder you were able to pin me so quickly. I was beginning to question my skills and training." Holy shit. The woman was a Valkyrie. Rather than intimidate him, it made him admire her even more. "I'm impressed."

"Don't be. It was a means to an end."

"Did it pay that well?"

She shrugged. "I wasn't in it for the money."

"No?" He tilted his head to the side. "Then why?"

Danny turned away and walked to the window. "I needed an outlet for pent-up...energy."

If he wasn't mistaken, she'd meant to say another word, not energy and had opted at the last second to change it. He'd bet she'd meant to say anger or frustration. As she stood framed in the window, wearing the dark blue dress, her sandy-blond hair pulled up in a messy bun at the base of her skull, she radiated frustration and constrained energy with nowhere to burn it off.

"I get it," he said softly. "When I feel that way, I run until I can't run another step."

"Yeah, well, running wasn't enough." She clenched her fists. "I needed more. I needed the physical challenge of getting in shape and learning the skills needed to compete."

"And when working out didn't do it, you entered the ring?"

She looked over her shoulder at him. "Something like that."

"And did it help?"

She nodded. "It did."

"Then why did you leave it? Other than your family wanting you to play bodyguard for your uncle."

Her lips pressed together. "After a while, pounding my opponents into submission got old. They weren't the people I really wanted to hurt. I finally realized that I'd never get that opportunity, and I just had to accept that."

Smoke crossed the room to stand closer to her. The woman might be a kickass MMA fighter, but at that moment, in that dress that showed off her gentle curves and toned body, she appeared vulnerable. Smoke figured she'd hear that word as a challenge if he dared to speak it aloud in reference to her. "Who did you want to hurt, if not your opponent?" he asked softly.

She didn't look around at him, instead of focusing on the window and the lights from the streetlamps. "It doesn't matter," she whispered. "That part of my life is over and done. There's no going back, only going forward."

He studied her face in the reflection from the glass.

The shadows beneath her eyes appeared darker in the window.

Smoke's chest tightened. The sudden urge to hit someone swelled in his chest. Someone had abused this woman, giving her that look of sadness, regret and residual anger. Whatever demons she'd fought in herself that had driven her to the MMA arena might have abated, but they weren't gone.

"Look," Smoke said, "I don't like the idea of masquerading as an engaged couple any more than you do, but now that your uncle has made the announcement, we might as well take advantage of the cover and make sure we're giving the same storyline."

She sighed. "He made it more complicated than it had to be. And I'm a terrible liar."

He smiled. "Then don't think of it as lying. Think of it as stealth operations. To blend into the environment and not stand out, you must camouflage. Our fake engagement is a kind of camouflage that will keep others from questioning why both of us are always hanging around the ambassador."

Danny faced him, her brow forming a V over her nose. "Are you going to make military analogies everywhere we go? If so, just shoot me now."

Smoke chuckled. "I've been married to the Army since I left high school. It's all I know."

"You know there's a whole other world out there besides the Army," she said.

He nodded. "I know. I like being a part of Delta Force. My team is my family."

"Lucky you," she said, her lips forming a thin line. "Not all units are as cohesive."

"True," he said. "I know how lucky I am. I figure I'll keep doing what I'm doing until I can't do it anymore."

"And then?" Danny cocked an eyebrow.

Smoke shrugged. "I have a piece of property in North Carolina. I'll build a house and grow a garden."

Her face softened. "That sounds nice. But what will you do for a job?"

"I might work at a hardware store. I like the smell of wood and paint. Or I could go into selling real estate. I remember how rewarding it was to find my little tract of land. Wouldn't it be nice to help others find their dream home? Or I could flip houses. I like working with my hands."

"Sounds a lot more productive than using your hands to beat others into submission." She shook her head. "Too many military folks come off active duty without a clue as to what they're going to do next and discover that finding that something is harder than they could've imagined."

"I've heard that," Smoke said. "Some of my friends who left the service are still trying to figure out what they want to do or how they fit into a civilian world. I don't want to be like that. I've already started thinking about what I want to do when I'm no longer in the Army."

"Smart," she said.

"Did you know you were headed for the MMA circuit when you left active duty?" he asked.

Danny laughed. "Hardly. I kind of fell into it. I was seeing a counselor for PTSD. She suggested I get a personal trainer to get in shape and learn self-defense to build confidence." She shook her head. "I worked hard, learned fast and caught the attention of a scout. The next thing I knew, I was fighting for money."

"And if you had it to do again, would you have chosen the path you took?" he asked.

Her chin lifted. "Knowing what I know now? Absolutely. I wouldn't be where I am today, both physically and mentally. I needed that time in the MMA to realize what I was capable of. Now, I'm stronger than I was in the Army and more confident in my ability to defend myself. I wouldn't have gotten this far without having challenged myself and others in the arena."

"Then you're one of the success stories." He grinned. "Congratulations."

"Don't congratulate me yet. I don't know what's next for me. This is my first self-assignment as a bodyguard. It'll be a success if I keep my uncle alive and well, so he has the opportunity to live into his old age."

"Do you think you'll continue as a bodyguard after your uncle no longer needs you?" he asked.

She shook her head. "I don't know. Ask me when I've succeeded at this tasking." She shot a crooked smile in his direction. "My uncle is my family. I love him and want to help him as much as possible."

"He loves you, too," Smoke said with a grin. "He warned me not to hurt you."

Her brow furrowed. "Not hurt me? Doesn't he realize I can take care of myself?"

Smoke laughed out loud. "I wanted to laugh when he said that. Especially knowing firsthand what you're capable of. I have a bruised backside and sore arm to prove it." His grin faded. "He was quick to clarify that the kind of hurt he was talking about was more mental than physical."

Her mouth formed a tight frown. "You can't hurt me," she said. "I consider myself immune to most smooth-talking men whose boot sizes are larger than their IQs. I'm not going to be hurt. I haven't met a man yet who could touch me mentally." Her chin rose higher with each word until she looked down her nose at Smoke's chest. "Since I left the Army, I haven't met a man who could hurt me physically. Not again."

"You speak from experience?" he asked.

She nodded. "More than I care to admit or relive," she leaned forward. "Are we ready to go into the lion's den?"

Smoke met her gaze, shaking his head. "I can do this alone. You don't have to perform the body-guard function."

"The hell I don't," Danny bristled. "He's my uncle. Where he goes, I'll go. End of subject." She walked past him and paced the floor of the apart-ment. "What we need to do now is craft our story."

"We met in…" Smoke gave Danny the opportu-nity to fill in the blank.

"What?" she asked. Her eyes widened, and she nodded. "Where would we have met?" she asked. "When you're not deployed, you're at Ft Bragg, North Carolina."

"We could've met aboard a cruise ship," Smoke offered.

"That's not something I would do," she said. "My friends know I'm not a big fan of cruises."

"How about we met at a bowling alley outside of Fort Bragg?" he asked. "Or, don't tell me…you don't bowl."

Danny grinned. "Sorry, I don't bowl. I can play a mean game of tennis when I have time. But no on the bowling alley."

Smoke crossed his arms over his chest. "What do you suggest?"

"Why don't we stick as close to the truth as possible?" she said.

"Okay..." Smoke's eyes narrowed. "I came to your uncle's office. You saw me. I flipped over you, and your uncle introduced us."

Danny's lips twitched. "I like it. And all of it is true." She straightened her shoulders and lifted her chin. "That's all good. At least we have a room for tonight."

"What about our engagement?" Smoke asked. "Did I pop the question over dinner? Did I fly all the way to Israel to ask for your hand? Or did you ask me? I'm all about equal opportunity when it comes to proposing."

"You flew to Israel and asked me as soon as you saw me," Danny said.

"Nothing on a billboard or pulled on a long sign behind an airplane?" he asked.

Danny shook her head. "All good ideas. But you know me well. I don't go for the fancy stuff. Just a knee and a question."

"And the ring didn't fit, so we're having it sized." He nodded. "Do we plan on having kids?"

Her forehead wrinkled. "Do we have to go into that much detail?" she asked.

"Someone is bound to ask," he said.

"Fine." Danny shot a glance to the empty corner in the ceiling. "We both want children. A boy and a girl."

"We won't stop having babies until we have at least one of each." He grinned. "Your idea."

"Where are we getting married?" she asked.

"In Vegas when we both are back in the States."

"At an Elvis chapel," Danny said. "I've always dreamed of having my wedding officiated by an Elvis impersonator."

"I always wanted to marry someone with a sense of humor." His smile broadened. "Someone who would think it great to be married by an Elvis impersonator."

She nodded. "Life's too short not to have a sense of humor."

"Agreed," Smoke said.

"I had to find mine after having lost it for a while." She crossed her arms over her chest. "My favorite color is sapphire blue."

"Easy to remember," Smoke said. "I'll just remember how beautiful you were tonight in that dress."

Her cheeks turned red, and she glanced away. "My favorite flowers are—"

He held up his hand. "Let me guess. Daisies?"

She shook her head. "Tulips because they remind me of spring."

Smoke gave a slight nod. "Good choice. Have you been to the Netherlands when the tulips are blooming?"

Danny shook her head. "No. But it's on my bucket list."

"We'll go there on our honeymoon," Smoke said. "Which means we're getting married in April of next year."

"What else would someone ask?" Danny tapped her finger against her chin.

"What attracted you to me and vice versus," Smoke suggested.

Danny tipped her head to one side. "Your smile," she grinned. "Even when I'm kicking your ass."

He stepped close to her and stared down into her eyes. He wanted to touch her, to smooth the hair back from her face and brush his lips across hers. "I was attracted to you from your first touch. But it was your gray-blue eyes that seem to look past my bullshit straight into my soul that won me over."

For a long moment, her gaze met his. He could swear she swayed toward him, if ever so slightly. All he'd have to do was lower his head, and he could claim her lips in a kiss.

Her chin lifted, and her eyelids lowered for a second.

Then they opened wide, and she stepped back. "I think that's enough to remember," she said. "We have a busy day tomorrow. My uncle is visiting outlying villages. We'll accompany him. I'm sure he'll want you to come along and maybe some of your team. I suggest you get some sleep. It'll be a long day."

Smoke stepped up to her, his gaze capturing hers all over again. "You felt it, too, didn't you?"

"I...I don't know what you're talking about," she said, her voice not much more than a whisper.

"The magnetism between you and me. You felt it." He raised his hand and caught himself before laying it on her cheek. It remained upraised an inch from touching her skin. It took all his self-control to stop short of crossing that line. "Even if you don't admit it, I will. I want to touch you, to kiss you and hold you close."

Her chest rose and fell as her breathing became more rapid and ragged.

"But I won't do those things unless you ask for them. I shouldn't even be thinking about them, considering you are my assignment, but I'd be willing to break all the rules to kiss you just once."

Smoke sighed, dropped his hand to his side and stepped back. "Go to sleep, dear Danica. Dream of our engagement and how I wanted so badly to kiss you."

He spun on his heel and marched for the door. He paused with his hand on the knob and turned back. "My favorite color is gray-blue, the color of your eyes."

She stood transfixed. Her mouth opened as if to say something then snapped closed.

Smoke left her there, closing the door softly behind him. He waited a full minute until he heard the reassuring sound of the deadbolt clicking into place.

A smile spread across his face as he walked to the next door down the hall from Danny's. So much for remaining hands-off. Danica Turner was an amazing woman, one he wanted to get to know beyond her favorite color and flower. He wanted to know what made her cry out in passion and lose herself making love.

When they'd been given their orders to report to the embassy, he'd assumed it was a punishment for the disaster of their mission into Gaza. He'd been sure he'd be bored out of his mind within the first thirty minutes. He hadn't expected to be tackled and pinned by a gray-eyed temptress in a dark blue dress that hugged every inch of her body like he'd like to.

This assignment just got a whole lot more complicated than he'd originally expected.

Smoke was definitely up for the challenge.

CHAPTER 4

DANNY SLEPT FITFULLY, waking well before dawn, tired. Every time she drifted into sleep, she dreamed of a ruggedly handsome man standing at the end of a chapel aisle with Elvis beside him, waiting for her to join him. And every time, she wanted to go to him, but her feet wouldn't move. Arms reached out from behind her. Gnarly fingers grasped her wedding dress and pulled her back, ripping the lace and veil.

When she woke in the gray light of pre-dawn, she got up. Since sleep wasn't restful, she figured a workout would be more beneficial.

She changed into shorts, a sports bra and slipped into her running shoes. After she pulled her hair up into a ponytail high on the crown of her head, she left her room and hurried to the exercise center in the basement of the building.

After years of hard training to get her body into peak condition for the MMA circuit, she craved exercise and didn't feel good until she'd run several miles and challenged her muscles with strenuous weight training each day.

Usually, she was the first one down. She liked working out on her own with no one to interrupt her concentration with talk and no one watching her. She frowned when she heard the steady pounding of someone running on one of the few treadmills the center offered. Danny sighed and pushed open the door to the room.

The man on the treadmill made Danny's heart flutter. Damn. What was it about Asher Gray that made her knees weak and her pulse pound? The man was nicknamed right. Where there was Smoke, there was fire.

As soon as the thought surfaced in her mind, her cheeks heated as if she stood in front of a blazing bonfire. Yeah. The man inspired fire.

Danny turned to leave, afraid that if she stayed, she might get burned.

"Danny," his voice called out.

Damn. She'd been spotted.

She forced herself to turn back with a neutral look on her face. "Oh, Smoke. It's you. I wasn't sure, and I didn't want to interrupt your workout."

He kept running at a swift pace, never slowing. A smile crossed his lips. The man had barely even broken a sweat. "I'm almost done," he said. "On the treadmill. I'll move to the weights next."

She nodded, completely familiar with the machines and their functionality, having been there for a number of weeks and working out daily. She grabbed one of the small towels from the stack near the door, looped it over the handrails on one of the treadmills, stepped up onto the sides and started the belt. After she bumped it up to the speed she preferred, she hopped on and started out in a slow jog to warm up.

"I'm glad we can talk before the day begins," Smoke said, continuing his run as if talking had no impact on his lung capacity.

After a tenth of a mile warmup, Danny knocked the speed up several notches until she was stretching her legs to keep up with the pace of the belt. Still, she wasn't running nearly as fast as Smoke—and she considered herself to be in excellent shape.

Her competitive streak pushed her to go faster, ramping up the belt speed until she was moving along as quickly as Smoke. For the first five minutes, she did great. The next five minutes and thirty-seven seconds, not so great.

"I thought you said you were almost done," she said, trying hard not to wheeze as she sucked air into her starving lungs.

"I am. Only two more miles, and I'll move on to weights."

"Only two…" She frowned, her breath coming in ragged spurts. "How many miles do you run?"

"Between six and eight. Depends on how much time I have for the workout." He kept up the pace, a slight sheen of perspiration making his forehead shine.

Fifteen minutes into her run, Danny was forced to slow the belt or fly off when she passed out. She hated to admit the man was in better shape for long distances than she was. She only had to be able to run far enough to get out of a bad situation. Danny felt no burning desire to run marathons or even half-marathons. Her purpose for getting in shape and learning martial arts was to be physically and mentally prepared if someone attacked her…again. She refused to be subjected to the horrifying brutality of any man bent on slaking his desires on an unwilling victim.

Finally, Smoke slowed his machine until he was walking, and then came to a stop. He stepped off the belt and looped his towel around his neck. "How much longer are you going?" he asked.

Danny wished she'd lasted a few more minutes at high speed but couldn't totally regret slowing down. At least now, she could breathe normally. "I'll go another ten minutes."

"Do you lift weights?" His gaze skimmed over

her bare arms. "Of course, you do weights. We can talk then."

Did they have to talk at all? Danny kept that thought to herself. Her unwilling attraction to the man could be a distraction in her effort to protect her uncle from threats. She supposed they'd have to establish some kind of working relationship to keep up their cover and so that they weren't duplicating effort or letting some things fall through the cracks, thinking the other was handling it. She nodded and kept running.

When she left the treadmill, she moved to the weight equipment where she'd learned to work every muscle in her body using various apparatus and free weights. She was in the middle of leg pressing two-hundred and fifty pounds when Smoke spoke again.

"I understand your uncle is scheduled to visit the border towns close to the Palestinian Territories today. What are your thoughts?" He curled twenty-five-pound dumbbells, his muscles bulging as he worked the weights.

Danny's mouth was suddenly dry. She swallowed hard and concentrated on what he'd said, not what he was doing. "What do you mean?" she asked, bending her knees and then flexing them again.

"Is it a good idea to be that close to the territories when they're blaming the US for the rocket explosion that took out a portion of one of the medical facilities in Gaza?"

She paused with her legs extended. "Who said it was a rocket explosion? From what my uncle said, the US and the Israelis haven't fired any rockets into Gaza lately." Her eyes narrowed. "Do you know something we don't know?"

He paused for a nanosecond then continued curling the weights out and back. "From the sound of the damage, I assumed the explosion was caused by a rocket."

"If the US and Israel didn't fire the rocket, who did?" she asked.

"Our intelligence sources reported rockets being fired from inside Gaza out to Israeli-held territory. Why not Hamas or other Palestinians?" he asked. Smoke set the dumbbells on the caddy and moved to the bench press.

"Why would they fire their rockets into their own city?" Danny asked.

Smoke shrugged. "What if it was an accident?"

Danny's head tipped to one side. "It makes for a great story the Hamas can twist for their own purposes."

Smoke nodded. "So, do you think it's a good idea for your uncle to venture near the border towns close to the Palestinian territory border?" He lifted a barbell with over four hundred pounds of free weights from their resting place, lowered it to his chest then raised it again. He did this several times.

Danny held her breath while he bench-pressed the weight. If he got into trouble, she'd be of no assistance. She couldn't lift four hundred pounds. The best she'd been able to do was two hundred and twenty-five. Even then, she'd had a spotter on standby to help her if she needed it.

When he placed the weights on the metal rests and sat up, she let go of the breath she'd been holding.

By that time, the Delta's body had a thin coat of perspiration, making his skin shine like a model for a men's fitness magazine.

It had been a long time since Danny had felt anything like desire for a man. Why all of a sudden this one? When she'd worked with a physical trainer at a gym, she'd been around several weight-lifting men with bulging muscles and hadn't been the least bit attracted to them.

Smoke was different. He didn't appear to be bulking up for the sake of showing off his muscles, like so many men she'd met at the gym. He went after his workout with purpose. His shoulders were broad, and he sported the coveted six-pack abs. But he wasn't hugely bulky to the point he'd have to have his uniforms specially tailored to fit. He was… just right.

Danny dragged her gaze from him, pumped out

ten more repetitions than she usually did, and then moved on to the next machine. "My uncle understands the dangers and the need to get out and meet the people of the country in which he has established diplomatic relations. I'm also sure he'll have an escort to see to our safety."

Smoke shot a glance her way. "You're going, too?" He rose from the bench, frowning.

"Of course." Danny grabbed the twenty-five-pound dumbbells and sat on the bench Smoke had vacated. She laid back and pressed the dumbbells. "I came to Israel to protect and help my uncle. I can't do that unless I'm with him."

"I'll be there," Smoke pointed out.

"Good. Then he'll have even more coverage," she said without glancing in his direction. "In the past, my Aunt Ruth went with him to meet the people. She passed away six months ago. I'm not only the ambassador's undeclared bodyguard; I'm my aunt's stand-in."

Smoke nodded. "That makes sense. And it makes sense for me to accompany my fiancée and her uncle. I've arranged for half of my team to accompany your uncle on his visit. We're taking two SUVs."

Danny sat up with a smile. "Good. I'll feel better knowing we have backup." And she'd be spending the day with the man who was playing havoc with the libido she'd never thought would revive from the trauma she'd experienced in the Army. Great. She wasn't sure how she felt about this man she had to pretend was her fiancé. He made her feel slightly off-balance every time he was near.

Danny pushed to her feet, still holding twenty-five-pound weights in each hand. When she swung toward the caddy where the weights were stacked, she stumbled, dropped the dumbbells and almost fell, if not for a pair of hands reaching out to catch her.

Smoke grabbed her around the waist and hauled her back up against his front.

For a long moment, she stood still, the hard planes of his chest pressing into her back, solid arms wrapped around her, steadying her.

She held her breath and waited for the panic that normally overcame her when men touched her.

It didn't come. In its place was that heat that started at her core and flared throughout her body.

Danny drew in a breath, then another, her chest rising and falling, her hands lowering to rest on his arms.

"Are you alright?" he asked, his voice deep, resonating from his chest into hers.

Danny could do no more than nod, glad her back was to him so that he couldn't see the range of emotions she was certain were flooding her face. "I'm fine."

His arms loosened.

Still, she didn't step free of them. She liked how they made her feel safe.

Safe.

Her brow lowered. She'd learned the only person who could keep her safe was herself. She'd trained hard to make that true.

Her chin came up, and she pushed free of Smoke's arms. "I'm not usually this clumsy," she said. "Thank you."

He dipped his head. "My pleasure."

She glanced around, unsure where she'd left off, and suddenly didn't care. She just needed to put some space between herself and Smoke before she did something stupid. She didn't even want to put a name to what might be stupid. Any number of things came to mind all too quickly. None of which would be a good idea. "I'm headed back to my quarters. My uncle should be stirring. I want to be there when he's ready to go down to breakfast."

He tossed his towel into the laundry hamper. "I'm headed that way myself."

So much for getting away from the man.

Danny dropped her towel in the hamper and hurried for the door. The sooner she was back in her apartment, the sooner she could be away from Smoke and his magnetic effect on her. As much as she tried not to be, she was attracted to the man. Not good. Not good at all.

CHAPTER 5

SMOKE ACCOMPANIED Danny on the climb up the stairs from the basement to the floor where their apartments were located.

He waited as Danny fit her key into the lock on her door and pushed through. She turned and gave him a brief smile. "Breakfast is in fifteen minutes."

"I'll be ready," he said, waiting for her to close her door before he left.

She stood for a moment, opened her mouth, and then closed it and closed the door quickly. The click of the lock assured him she'd locked the door.

Smoke wondered what it was she'd wanted to say but hadn't. Danica Turner, for all her MMA fighting experience, seemed a bit hesitant around him. Did he scare her?

He shook his head. No way. The woman could take down a grown man in two seconds. She had nothing to fear. Her uncle had insinuated she'd been traumatized while on active duty in the Army. Had he frightened her by grabbing her to keep her from falling?

His gut knotted. Was she afraid he'd attack her like someone else probably had?

The thought made him feel awful. He'd never harm a woman. And he had enough respect already for Danny that he'd never do anything to make her feel uncomfortable. As much as he'd loved the feel of her body against his, he'd be careful not to do anything that would trigger her into a panic attack.

Hell. The thought of anyone hurting Danny made anger burn deep inside Smoke. If he could, he'd send her back to the States where she'd be safe from the fighting going on between Hamas and the Israelis. The people in the foreign service placed themselves in danger on a daily basis and risked being caught in the crossfire.

Who was he kidding? He couldn't force her to go back to the States. He had no control over her. She was there for her uncle. Smoke couldn't see her abandoning the ambassador because things got a little dicey. If he stayed, she'd stay.

Smoke entered his room, stripping as he made his way to the bathroom. He was showered, shaved and dressed in ten minutes and waiting outside Danny's door.

Her uncle emerged from his apartment before Danny.

"Good morning, Mr. Gray," he boomed.

Smoke moved toward the man, his hand outstretched. "Good morning, Ambassador Turner."

"Please, call me James," the older man said.

"Yes, sir." He grinned. "James."

The ambassador nodded his approval. "My niece isn't ready? She's always ready before me."

"I might've delayed her during her workout. She should be ready any moment."

As if on cue, Danny's door opened and she stepped out, wearing a sundress with a yellow and white daisy pattern sprinkled over the cornflower blue background. She'd left her sandy-blond hair hanging down around her shoulders, making her appear much younger than her thirty years. He held out a hand to her.

She placed her palm on his.

"You look gorgeous," he said, drawing her closer, without touching her body with his.

Color flooded her cheeks. "Thank you." Her gaze traveled his length. "You don't look bad, yourself."

He wore dark trousers, a white polo shirt and a black leather belt, the only nice outfit he'd brought when he'd packed his go bag for deployment to Jerusalem.

The ambassador chuckled, reminding Smoke that he and Danny weren't alone. "I take it you two ironed out all the details of your engagement?"

They faced the older man together.

"Yes, sir," Smoke said. "We met in your office a while back."

"He fell for me," Danny said, a smile tilting her lips. "He flew all the way to Israel because he couldn't stand another moment without me and proposed as soon as he arrived."

Her uncle grinned. "Perfect. I almost believe it myself." He held out his arm. "Shall we?"

Danny released Smoke's hand and slipped her hand into the crook of her uncle's elbow. "Yes. I'm starving."

"Worked up an appetite in the gym?" the ambassador asked as he started down the staircase.

"I most certainly did," she said, casting a glance over her shoulder at Smoke following a few steps behind them.

"Good. You'll want a good breakfast," Ambassador Turner said. "We have a long day ahead. We're going out to visit some of the outlying villages. I'd like to talk with some of the people and hear their concerns."

"Are you sure now is a good time to be out in the open?" Danny asked.

Smoke grinned. She had been listening to his own worries about their planned activities.

"These villages are on the edge in more ways than one. I understand some of them were hit by rockets launched out of Gaza two nights ago. The same night as the explosion that damaged the medical facility in Gaza. I like to think the explosion in Gaza ended the rocket attack sooner than Hamas planned."

Smoke wondered if the ambassador knew more than he was letting on. Had someone briefed him on the activities his team had participated in prior to arriving at the embassy?

The mission, as most of those the Deltas conducted, had been top secret. Smoke wasn't authorized to say anything about it. And he wouldn't.

At breakfast, some of the young women asked Danny about the proposal and where they planned to get married. As Danny answered with the story they'd concocted, she looked across the table at him, a smile playing across her lips.

Her look hit him square in the gut, and he found himself almost wishing their story wasn't a story at all. He could imagine actually standing in front of Elvis with her at his side. He'd smile like a fool, happiness radiating out of every pore. He liked humor and enjoyed the music Elvis had produced. His mother had been a big fan and had played his songs throughout Smoke's childhood. It was somewhat of a tradition for his family to be

Elvis fans, going back to when his grandparents had been young adults during the 1950s and 60s. He hoped his children would carry on the tradition and keep the King alive through a love of his music.

Children.

His chest tightened.

Throughout his career in the Army, he hadn't really considered marriage and children. There had never seemed to be time or the right circumstances. Namely, a woman he would contemplate marrying. Yet, he sat across the breakfast table in the US embassy in Jerusalem, picturing a scenario so foreign to his way of life and with a woman who was practically a stranger.

Danny leaned toward him. "What are you smiling about?"

Heat rose up his neck. "Nothing. I'm just happy to be here with you," he said for the benefit of the women who'd been questioning Danny about the proposal and wedding plans. He found the words easy to say and realized they weren't a lie.

Danny blushed. "I'm glad you're here, too."

After breakfast, they returned to their rooms to brush their teeth and prepare for their trip to the outlying villages.

"Meet me in my office in fifteen minutes," the ambassador said.

"Yes, sir." Smoke left the man at his door and Danny at hers before he continued on to his.

Once inside his apartment, he took the opportunity to contact Ketch on his cellphone.

Ketch answered on the first ring. "About time you checked in."

"I've been busy," Smoke said.

"You'll have to fill us in on how busy," Ketch said. "I understand some of us are accompanying you today."

"That's what I hear," Smoke said. "We can talk more then."

"Gotcha," Ketch said. "See ya in a few."

Smoke ended the call.

He'd wanted to say so much more, but he didn't want to risk the chance of their cellphone calls being intercepted. They might be a little paranoid, but as his former commander had always said, better paranoid than dead.

He exited his apartment at the same time as Danny. Together, they descended the stairs to the ground level and hurried to the ambassador's office. His door was open, and his secretary stood over his shoulder, handing him documents to be signed, one at a time. When he'd scratched his signature on the last page, he handed it back to the secretary and she left the room, smiling as she went.

"Had to get a little work done. This place doesn't run itself." The man pushed to his feet and joined them at the door. "Are you ready?"

Danny nodded.

"Yes, sir," Smoke said.

They stepped out of the front entrance of the embassy where two large SUVs stood along with three of the Deltas from Smoke's team, dressed in slacks and polo shirts. Without their body armor, helmets and weapons, they looked like men of leisure, ready for a day touring the countryside.

"Ambassador Turner," Smoke said. "Let me introduce my business associates." He waved toward the man closest to him, Quintin "Ice" Moore, with dark brown hair and ice-blue eyes, otherwise known as Ice because of the color of his eyes and his ability to freeze someone out with a stare. Rather than call them by the names anyone could look up in their military records, Smoke gave another name. "Clint Morris."

As the two men shook hands, Smoke waved toward the next man, Beau Guidry, with black hair and brown eyes and an unmistakable Cajun accent that had gotten him tagged with his moniker Voodoo early in his career. "Bob Giles, Ambassador Turner."

"And last but not least, Kirk Kassavich." Ketch fought the grin threatening to fill his face as his teammate shook hands with the diplomat. Karl Ketchum was the oldest of the team, the more experienced Delta. He shook the ambassador's hand. "Pleased to meet you, sir."

Smoke turned to Danny. "Gentlemen, I'd like to introduce you to the reason I came all the way to Israel. This beautiful young lady is Danica Turner, the woman who has graciously agreed to become my wife."

Smoke almost laughed out loud at the expressions of shock on his teammates' faces.

Ketch was the first to pull himself together. He pounded Smoke on his back. "Congratulations, man. Why didn't you tell us you were coming all the way out here to find a bride?"

Ice shook his head and held out his hand to Danny. "I hope you know what you're getting yourself into. Just know, if things don't work out between you, I'm thirty, single and available." He winked. "Really. Congratulations. You couldn't have picked a better man."

Danny's cheeks turned red and stayed red as each of Smoke's teammates shook her hand and congratulated her. "Thank you," she said. "It was all a surprise to me."

"Us, too. I thought we were here on vacation with our good buddy, Ash," Voodoo said. "Who knew?"

The Ambassador made eye contact with each man. "I trust you have found Jerusalem to be beautiful and friendly?"

"Yes, sir," the three men answered as one.

The ambassador went on. "I understand the

others in your party have found something more interesting to do than follow us around the countryside."

"Yes, sir," Ketch said. "We're the more adventurous of the group."

"We're happy to have you along for the ride." Ambassador Turner waved toward the SUVs. "Let's get this show on the road. We have a lot of ground to cover in a short amount of time."

Smoke, Danny and the Ambassador climbed into the lead SUV. Smoke took the passenger seat beside the young Marine driver who was dressed in a camouflage uniform. The other three Deltas loaded into the other SUV. Ketch rode shotgun with another Marine driver.

"What do you hope to accomplish with this visit?" Danny asked her uncle as they sped along the highway, heading west out of Jerusalem and north.

"I want to talk with Israelis in the areas along the border of the Palestinian territory," Ambassador Turner said. "Then I want to talk with the Palestinians. I'd like to get both sides of the story, so to speak. It might help in negotiations between them. At the very least, I want them to know I'm listening."

They spent the morning in a small village of Israelis to the north of Tel Aviv. They were welcomed with smiles and open arms and were shown around the village to the modern amenities that had been built along with a planned subdivision of houses.

As they drove across to the Palestinian line, they were welcomed with suspicion and narrow-eyed glares. Ambassador Turner spoke softly and listened to their concerns about Jewish encroachment on Palestinian territory. They feared that if the encroachment continued, and nothing was done to stop it, there would be no place for the Palestinians to go.

As they spoke with a few men, more gathered until a crowd surrounded the ambassador.

"Sir," Smoke touched the man's arm, "it's time to go."

Ambassador Turner nodded and spoke aloud. "I'll share your concerns with the Israeli government."

"They will not listen," one man said. "They disrupt our supply chain and access to good medical care."

Another man shook his fist in the air. "They will steal our land, kill our children and drive us from our own country."

"What will you do but side with the Israelis?" The man spat at the ambassador's feet.

Smoke started forward, his fists clenched, wishing he had a weapon.

The ambassador touched his arm, holding him

back. He nodded toward the man who'd spit. "Thank you for taking the time to speak with me. I am listening, and I've heard you." The ambassador moved toward the SUV.

The Deltas surrounded him and Danny, creating a small bubble of protection.

Had Smoke known they'd be completely surrounded and outnumbered ten to one, he would have insisted on a much larger escort. The air was thick with the crowd's hostility.

Once they reached the SUV, Smoke opened the door. "Get in," he said to Danny.

"After the ambassador," she said and stood to the side, waiting for her uncle to get in first.

The older man glanced over his shoulder once more before he bent to get in.

A sudden movement to Smoke's left drew his attention.

A man burst through the Deltas and rushed toward the ambassador, wielding a knife with a wicked long blade.

Before Smoke could react, Danny, in her blue dress with the pretty white daisy print, the closest person to the attacker, spun sideways, bent at the knees and thrust her leg out in a sideways kick that landed in the man's belly, sending him flying backward into the crowd.

Smoke gave the ambassador a hefty shove, sending him flying into the vehicle, grabbed Danny, lifted her off her feet and tossed her in behind him, closing the door once she was inside.

"Go!" he called out to his teammates as he hopped into the passenger seat and hit the lock button.

The Marine driver had already shifted into drive, easing forward through the crowd. He stopped when the men refused to move out of the way.

"Go!" Smoke urged.

"What if they won't move?" the young Marine said.

"Either they move, or they get run over."

The Marine started forward again.

Men climbed onto the hood of the SUV, pounding their fists against the windshield. One man leaped onto the hood with a hammer and slammed it into the glass, shattering it.

"Hit the accelerator," Smoke commanded.

The crowd parted, but the men on the hood refused to get off.

The marine punched the accelerator sending the SUV shooting forward.

"Hang on!" Smoke grabbed the steering wheel and yanked it to the right, and then back to the left. Two of the men slid off, falling to the ground.

Another man ran alongside the car, carrying a heavy pipe. He smashed it against the back window, completely shattering the glass.

Smoke spun in his seat. "Danny!"

"I'm all right," she called out.

When the man with the pipe flung himself through the opening, Danny leaned back against the ambassador and kicked with both feet, connecting with the man's face. The man flew backward and out of the window, landing on the ground outside.

The man with the hammer, hanging onto the hood, swung again. The hammer smashed through the glass and lodged halfway through.

"You know what to do," Smoke said to the Marine.

"Yes, sir." He jerked the steering wheel to the left then back to the right. The man on the hood clung to the hammer handle, his body sliding left then right.

"Again," Smoke yelled.

The Marine swerved sharply left then right. The man lost his grip on the hammer's handle and slid off the right side of the SUV, crashing to the ground.

Finally free of the mob, the Marine gunned the accelerator and drove back across the border to the Israeli side.

Smoke looked back to see the reassuring sight of the second SUV several car-lengths behind them, quickly catching up.

When they'd put sufficient distance between

them and the mob, and they were well into the Israeli territory, Smoke had the Marine pull to the side of the road. He dropped down, opened the back door and held out a hand to Danny.

She reached for his hand and let him pull her out of the vehicle and into his arms.

The second SUV came to a halt behind them, and everyone got out.

Ketch was first to get to their SUV. "Ambassador Turner?"

The ambassador climbed out of the SUV. "I'm fine. Is everyone else?"

Smoke looked around at the others. As far as he could tell, no one had been injured in the skirmish.

"Ms. Turner," Ketch frowned and nodded toward her leg. "You're bleeding."

She glanced down at the trail of blood dripping down the side of her calf and laughed. "Wow. I didn't even realize I'd been cut. Must've been the knife." She frowned. "I hope it doesn't stain."

Smoke shook his head, bent and scooped her up in his arms.

"It's just a scratch," she protested. "I can walk."

He nodded toward Ketch. "I believe there's a first aid kit in the back of each SUV."

Ketch ran to the back of the vehicle and opened the hatch.

Smoke followed Ketch and settled Danny in the back, her leg dangling over the edge.

Ketch had the first aid kit open and an alcohol swab torn from its packet. He started to hand it to Smoke.

"Not enough," Smoke said. He reached past Ketch for a gauze pad and the small bottle of rubbing alcohol. He doused the pad and bent to clean the wound. "It's gonna sting," he warned.

"I've had worse cuts in the MMA ring," Danny said. "I can handle this myself, you know."

Smoke pressed his lips together. "Humor me."

She sighed. "Just do it."

He cleaned the wound with the soaked pad and washed away the line of blood that had dripped down her leg. Then he poured alcohol over the wound and applied a dressing, securing it with medical tape. When he was done, he straightened, scooped her in his arms and carried her to the back seat of the SUV.

"Seriously, I can walk. It was just a little scratch."

"I know. I saw it. But how often do I get a chance to carry a kickass female, who could level me with her glare?" He winked as he settled her on the seat and brushed a kiss across her forehead. "I'm impressed, Danica Turner. Your uncle was right. You have some mad skills."

Her cheeks flushed a pretty pink. "He has to say nice things. He's my uncle."

"Maybe so. But you continue to prove him right. I'm beginning to think I'm superfluous."

She caught his arm. "We might not have gotten out of that situation had you and your friends not been there to assist. I'm good one-on-one. I doubt I'd be as adept against a crowd of angry men."

"I bet you'd do better than you think." He stared into her eyes. "The more I'm around you, the more I'm impressed. If I'm not careful, I could fall in love with you. Then I'm sure you'd kick my ass." He straightened and closed the door before he succumbed to the increasing desire to kiss her. Not on her forehead, but full-on, take her breath away, on her lips.

CHAPTER 6

DANNY SPENT the ride back to the embassy staring at the back of Smoke's head, wondering what it would have felt like had he kissed her lips instead of her forehead.

He'd taken the time to clean her wound and apply a proper dressing. His hands had been as gentle, if not more so, than a nurse's. All the while he'd touched her leg, her body had burned with the desire to have him touch her all over with those strong hands and firm fingers.

Smoke had definitely broken through the wall she'd built around her heart and feelings where it came to men. She'd really thought the sexual abuse she'd suffered at the hands of the platoon sergeant had ruined her for sex with any other male.

After she'd left the Army, she'd tried to date twice. Both times had ended terribly. When the guys had tried to kiss her good night, she'd shoved them away. The first one had kissed her on her doorstep. It had been easy to push him away, go inside and close the door in his face. The second guy had come onto her in his car. She'd told him to stop. When he hadn't, she'd gotten out and walked home. Neither man had called for a second date. Not that she would have gone out again with either one.

She'd truly thought she was done with the opposite sex and had resigned herself to living alone for the rest of her life. Her dream of having children would never happen unless she adopted or checked into a sperm bank for a donation to her pathetic cause.

Now...

Her heart raced and her core heated at the thought of Smoke's hands on her body. Hell, she sat beside her uncle, wicked thoughts of getting naked with the Delta roiling through her head. How messed up was that? And he didn't seem at all turned off by her ability to defend herself or that she'd taken him down when they'd first met.

The man's ego was intact. He'd even kissed her forehead and winked at her.

She leaned her head back against the seat and closed her eyes, imagining his lips on hers.

Danny opened her eyes and fought to get a grip. Just because he'd kissed her forehead, didn't mean he wanted to kiss any other part of her anatomy. He could just as easily have kissed a child on the forehead. It didn't mean anything. Cleaning her wound was the same. He'd have done it for anyone. Heck, he could have cleaned a wound on her uncle's leg with just as much care and concern. Granted, he probably wouldn't have kissed her uncle's forehead.

The thought made her lips twitch.

"What's so funny?" her uncle asked.

Danny's cheeks heated. "Nothing. I'm just glad we got out of there with no more casualties than we did."

"I hope no one got seriously hurt in the mob." Her uncle's brow furrowed. "I didn't mean to stir them up and add to the animosity. I only wanted to get a clear picture of both sides of the conflict."

"I know." Danny laid a hand on his. "You really try to do the right thing."

"Unfortunately, there are years of hard feelings and conflict between the people of this region."

Smoke turned in his seat to look back at the ambassador. "One person can't make that go away."

Again, the ambassador sighed. "But I have to understand the issues at the grassroots level to help in negotiations."

"I'd say you got a very clear understanding of how people feel today," Danny said.

Her uncle nodded and leaned back against his

seat. "I've always tried to make a difference in every assignment I've undertaken in the Foreign Service. Sometimes, I don't feel like I do enough."

"You're a good man, Uncle James. You care. So many people don't." She took his hand in hers and held it all the way back to the embassy.

Her uncle had the drivers go around to the rear entrance to the embassy. He didn't want the condition of the SUVs to cause an uproar among the staff, and he certainly didn't want news reporters to latch onto what had happened and make a bigger deal of it than it already was.

They'd gotten back late enough to have missed the regularly scheduled dinner.

"I'm tired. I'm going straight to bed," her uncle said as he climbed out of the SUV.

"Don't you want to get something to eat from the kitchen?" she asked. "I'm sure they saved a plate for you."

"I don't want to bother. A shower and a good night's sleep is what I want right now."

"Go on up. I'll bring you a sandwich," she said.

"I don't want you to go to the trouble," he said. "You must be tired as well. And you were injured."

"I'm fine," she assured him. "We missed lunch and dinner. I'm not going to bed without eating something and neither are you." When he started to argue, she shut him down. "I won't take no for an answer. I'll be up in a few minutes with a sandwich that you will eat."

He grinned. "You sound like your Aunt Ruth." His smile faded. "I miss her."

"I know." She hooked her arm through his and walked with him into the building. As she passed through the doorway, she glanced back.

Smoke stood with his teammates in deep conversation.

Danny was going to ask if he was coming but thought better of it. She didn't want to interrupt him. He hadn't had the opportunity to talk to his men alone since they'd set out that morning. He probably had a lot to catch up on.

The door closed slowly between them.

Danny sighed and turned to follow her uncle. So much for following through on all the sexual fantasies that had been mulling around in her head on the way back that evening. Perhaps it was better that they go to their corners and regroup before the next round. She wasn't sure she could handle anything more than a kiss to the forehead. She hadn't panicked or shoved him out the window like she had the man with the metal pipe. That didn't mean she wouldn't come unglued if he tried to go further with her. She might not be ready for the next step. And he might not have any desire to pursue anything with her. That thought was strangely depressing.

Behind her, the squeak of door hinges made her look back.

Smoke stood in the doorway. "Hey."

She smiled, a surge of joy rushing through her. "Hey."

"I need a few minutes with the guys. Will you and the ambassador be okay?"

She nodded. "We will. I'm going to get him settled and head to the kitchen. Do you want anything?"

He smiled a slow sexy smile before answering, "I'll join you there. I'm starving."

"Okay. I'll be there waiting for you. And making sandwiches because I'm hungry, too," she said and then clamped her mouth shut. She should have stopped at okay.

He smiled again. "I won't be long. And I can help." Then he was gone.

"You like him, don't you?"

Danny turned to find her uncle waiting in the hallway, a soft smile curving his lips. She gave him a weak smile. "Is it crazy that I do? I don't even know him."

Her uncle's smile broadened. "I knew I loved your Aunt Ruth from the moment I met her. It took her a couple of weeks to realize she loved me, too. I was persistent. She finally came around and admitted she loved me."

"And you two were together for how long?"

"Forty-four years, twenty-five days and six hours." He touched her cheek. "We packed a lot of love into that time. I always knew how lucky I was that she chose to be with me."

"You were blessed." Danny wondered if she would ever find that kind of love.

She fell into step beside her uncle and walked up the stairs to his apartment. Once he was settled, she left him and descended to the embassy kitchen. They had small kitchens in their apartments, but they rarely ate there. The embassy kitchen would have the leftovers from the staff's meal. If she wasn't mistaken, ham had been on the menu. She could make ham and cheese sandwiches for a quick, hearty meal.

Her pulse quickened as she pushed through the swinging door into the commercial kitchen. It wasn't fully lit like it was during meal preparations, but the staff always kept a single light on near the large commercial refrigerator for those who wanted a late-night snack.

Danny had hurried down, hoping to find Smoke already there. He wasn't. She swallowed her disappointment and told herself that she'd have time to find all the ingredients to make sandwiches. She dove into the refrigerator, locating a plastic container full of ham slices, cheese, a head of lettuce, a tomato and condiments. In the pantry, she found a loaf of bread and carried it out to the counter where she laid out six slices and began the assembly process. She layered ham, and then cheese, onto three slices of bread. She found a knife to cut the tomato and laid the slices on top of the cheese. She was tearing fat leaves off the head of lettuce when the kitchen door swung open. She fumbled the head and nearly dropped it, recovering before it hit the floor.

"Nice catch," Smoke said with a smile.

"Thanks," she said, heat rising into her cheeks. "I'm almost done. I just need to add the dressing. Mustard or mayo?"

"Both," he said. "Thank you."

She handed him the mustard and got out a knife to slather mayonnaise onto an empty slice of bread. After she applied the creamy white sauce, Smoke followed, adding mustard. "Do you like mustard as well?" he asked.

She nodded as she finished smoothing mayo over the second slice of bread and moved on to the last piece. "And so does the ambassador."

Smoke finished adding mustard on top of the mayonnaise and stepped back as Danny completed each sandwich with the last slice of bread. Then she wrapped each one in a paper towel and handed one to Smoke. "Do you want potato chips or something to drink to go with that?" she asked as she put away the ingredients.

After she slid the container of ham into the fridge, Smoke handed her the jar of mayonnaise and the mustard.

"No to the chips for me," Smoke said. "I'll have water. What about you?"

She took the knife to the sink, rinsed it and placed it in the dishwasher. Then she turned to face him. "I have water in my apartment. I doubt there's any in yours. You can get one from my room if you like." She gathered the last two sandwiches in her hands.

"Are you eating here or in your apartment?" he asked.

"I need to take one of these up to my uncle. I might as well eat in my apartment, rather than come all the way back down here." She took a breath and a leap. "Want to join me? Like I said, I have water bottles." That breath she'd taken lodged in her throat as she awaited his response.

He smiled. "I'd like that."

Her breath rushed out. Now that she'd invited him to join her, she had to get there. Breathing would help her climb the stairs.

Suddenly tongue-tied, she turned and headed out of the kitchen. Her heart pounded all the way up the stairs and had nothing to do with exertion and everything to do with hyperventilation. If she wasn't careful, she'd pass out before she got to her apartment with Smoke.

Her uncle answered the door on the first knock and smiled when he saw the sandwich in her hands. "Thank you, my dear. My stomach was rumbling, and I was thinking how wrong I was about going to bed on an empty stomach."

She handed him the sandwich. "Do you have something to drink with that?"

He nodded. "I do. Thank you again." He stepped back. "Do you want to come in and eat your sandwiches with me?"

Danny froze. She'd been so nervous about being alone in her apartment with Smoke, she hadn't thought her uncle might want company while he ate. How could she tell him she'd rather eat with Smoke? She opened her mouth with no idea what to say but was saved when her uncle frowned.

"On second thought," he said. "I might not be good company. I plan on eating and going right to sleep afterward."

"You've had an exhausting day," she rushed. "We wouldn't want to keep you chattering."

"Thank you for understanding." He raised his sandwich. "And thank you for taking care of me. Good night." He closed the door, leaving Danny and Smoke standing in the hallway.

Smoke chuckled. "He's a very intuitive man."

Danny glanced at Smoke's smiling face. "Why do you say that?"

"I think he really did want company for the meal."

Danny frowned. "Do you think he knew we were planning on eating in my room?"

"No, but the look of panic on your face probably gave him a clue."

Her cheeks burning, Danny turned toward her apartment, humiliated and filled with guilt for not wanting to have dinner with her uncle. "Was I that transparent?"

"Only to the trained eye," he said. "I think your uncle is skilled at reading people. You can't succeed as a diplomat if you can't read facial expressions and body language."

She opened the door to her apartment and stepped inside, glad she'd cleaned it that morning after her shower. Danny nodded toward the small dining table near the equally small kitchen. "Have a seat. I'll get the water bottles."

On her way through, she dropped her sandwich on the table and hurried for the refrigerator, needing to keep moving. Once she sat at the table, she'd be forced to come up with something interesting to say. What could that possibly be? She was stumped, tongue-tied and feeling completely inadequate. At thirty years old, she didn't have a clue how to be alone with a man. And she surely had no clue how to seduce one.

She was a woman. Shouldn't it come naturally?

With the two water bottles in hand, she walked slowly to the table, her thoughts pinging inside her head like the steel ball inside an antique pinball machine.

Smoke took both water bottles from her hands and set them on the table. "Hey," he said and tipped her chin up. "For a badass MMA fighter, you look like you want to run and hide somewhere. What's got you spooked?"

She laughed, "If only you knew, you'd be the one running."

"Try me," he said, taking her hands in his and urging her to take a seat at the table. He sat in front of her, still holding her hands, their knees touching. "If I didn't know better, I'd say you're afraid of me."

She shook her head. "Yes...and no." Then she sighed and stared at their hands. "Yes. I'm afraid. But not of you."

Smoke's brow wrinkled. He looked around the room. "If you aren't afraid of me, who are you afraid of?"

She gave him a wobbly smile. "Me. You should probably run now. I brought you here to seduce you."

His lips spread in a grin. "Is that so?"

Danny nodded, her cheeks burning. "You'll get a

kick out of this." She swallowed hard. "I don't know how, or if I'll have the courage to go through with…you know…sex." Deeply embarrassed by her confession, she couldn't meet his gaze. "You don't have to stay if you don't want to. I'll understand. You probably only wanted a bottle of water anyway."

"Stop," Smoke said gently, but firmly. "I could've gone straight to my room and eaten alone. I didn't because I wanted to be with you." He touched her cheek, urging her to look at him. "We've only known each other for a little more than twenty-four hours, and I'm intrigued."

"Ouch," she said. "Is intrigued like saying she's interesting? That word you use when you're trying to be polite?"

He shook his head. "Not at all." He brushed a strand of her hair back behind her ear. "When you tackled me in your uncle's office, I think I fell for you a little then."

"You fell, all right," she said.

"And it should've crushed my ego." He smiled. "But it didn't. I liked that you were a strong, feisty woman, capable of taking care of yourself and others. And that blue dress… Not only were you physically capable, but you were stunning. I admit, I came with you tonight to see where this was going." His brow dipped. "But I also want you to know, I won't do anything you don't want me to do. All you have to do is say stop, and I will. No pressure. I would never force myself on you."

Danny frowned. "Did my uncle say something about my time in the Army?"

Smoke shook his head. "Only that you had a difficult time in the military, and that I'd better not hurt you." He grinned. "Your uncle is looking out for you."

Her frown softened. "He's a good man. He takes care of so many. He and my Aunt Ruth were a good team. They set the example for what a married couple should be. And yes, I had a bad time of it on active duty."

"Please tell me justice was served." he said softly.

Danny nodded. "But not by the UCMJ. Though he was never convicted, the pending trial and negative press must've gotten to him. His wife left him, taking his kids halfway across the country. He committed suicide before his trial date."

Smoke's eyes narrowed. "That's just as well. It keeps me from killing him."

"I think they would've let him walk."

"Why do you say that?" Smoke asked.

"The Army doesn't like it when they get bad press. I was treated like the criminal. Like it was my fault. I was ruining a decorated soldier's career. Never mind he'd done it before. And who knows how many female soldiers suffered in silence? I wasn't the first, but I was the first to blow the whistle." She gave him a twisted smile. "How's that for baggage?"

"Sucks." He pulled her to her feet and held her hands in his. "If anything happens between us, you will be calling the shots."

She looked up into his eyes. "What if I don't know how? Before... what happened...I'd only fumbled around in the backseat of my boyfriend's car when I was in high school. He was so nervous, he couldn't..."

Smoke's brow descended. "You were a virgin when that bastard accosted you?"

She shrugged. "Yeah. But it didn't matter. Rape is rape."

Smoke wrapped his arms loosely around her and pulled her close.

If she wanted to get away, she could. She didn't.

Danny slipped her arms around his waist and rested her cheek against his chest. The rapid beat of his heart made her glance up.

He smiled down at her. "Yes, ma'am. You make my heart race."

She looked up into his eyes. "And I'm calling the shots?"

He nodded.

Her eyebrows drew together. "And you want this?"

He moved closer, the hard ridge of his cock pressing into her belly beneath the fabric of his trousers. "I've wanted you since you pinned me to the floor in your uncle's office and straddled me in that amazing blue dress."

"You have?" Her heart raced, matching the pace of his.

"Yes."

She drew in a breath, let it out and made her choice. "Will you show me how to make love?"

He pressed a kiss to her forehead. "It would be my pleasure," he said, his tone, deep, resonant and sexy as hell.

Emboldened by her decision, she lifted her chin and closed her eyes. "Can you start by kissing me on the lips?"

CHAPTER 7

SMOKE COULDN'T LIE to himself. He was almost afraid to make love to Danny. She'd placed a whole lot of trust in him to get it right. What if he did something that triggered her to panic or make her think she was being raped again? It was a huge amount of pressure for a guy who'd pleasured a number of women in his lifetime.

None of them had made it past three dates. He'd set that as his limit. After three dates, women became possessive.

Smoke had never met someone he wanted to commit to for the long haul. Not when he was still a part of Delta Force. He was married to his career. The missions always came first. He had yet to meet a woman who would understand that. And he wouldn't ask one to accept it. He was one of the few Deltas he knew who'd never married. Others had given it a shot and been burned when their wives had bailed on them after one or two deployments.

He'd considered himself lucky that he hadn't gotten caught in that trap. He didn't have to feel bad about leaving anyone behind, and he didn't have to worry that he'd get a Dear John letter while he was fighting for his country.

On the flip side of that argument, he didn't have anyone waiting for him to come home. When he returned from a deployment, he went back to his empty apartment outside of Fort Bragg, North Carolina. He'd walk through the door, dump his gear, do a little laundry and then wonder what to do next. He never stayed there long, preferring to hang out with his other unmarried or divorced teammates rather than stay in his apartment alone.

Now, standing in Danny's apartment, holding her in his arms, he wondered if maybe he'd been missing out on something special. He could imagine coming home to a woman, especially if she was a strong, independent woman, who could hold her own in a barroom fight and look like a million dollars in a dress or nothing at all. A woman like Danny. She'd been in the military and understood deployments.

She leaned back, her brow puckering. "Did my confessions kill the mood?"

"No. I'm just trying to decide how to proceed."

Danny shook her head. "Why don't we start by eating. That should give us time to think about what comes next."

Smoke nodded, letting her make the call even though the last thing on his mind was food. Getting naked was front and center, demanding his attention.

When she started to pull away, he tightened his hold on her. "Wait. Let me do one thing."

"What's that?" she asked.

He lowered his head and brushed his lips across hers, lightly, barely touching. He held back on the first pass.

Her hands slid up his chest and encircled the back of his neck, drawing him closer.

He increased the pressure on her lips, taking it slowly, not wanting to spook her.

When she opened her mouth to him, the dam on his control wavered and shook. He pulled back for half a second, and then claimed her lips, thrusting his tongue past her teeth to caress the length of hers.

She leaned into him, her chest pressed to his, that thin cornflower-blue sundress and his shirt the only barriers between them.

Normally, he'd have the woman naked by now. But this was Danny. He had to take it slowly or risk blowing it before they got started.

She lowered her hands to his chest and still

lower to the waistband of his trousers. She fumbled with his belt until he took matters in his own hands and freed the buckle.

Danny's fingers curled into his polo shirt, pulled it free of the trousers and pushed it up his torso.

He took it from there and pulled it over his head, letting it drop to the floor.

While he was shedding his shirt, she found the button on his trousers and worked it free. Her fingers wrapped around the zipper tab and pulled it downward.

He covered her hand before she'd gone halfway down. "Are you sure you want to move this fast?"

"I'd move a little faster with a little help," she said, her voice warm and husky.

He released her hand, and the zipper moved lower until his cock sprang free, jutting out straight and thick.

Danny's hand shook as her fingers wrapped around his shaft. "I don't know what to do," she said. "But I like this. Do you?" She looked up into his eyes.

"Darlin', yes." As much as he liked her hand on him, he wanted to show her how good it could be for her first. "But you need to know what good lovin' is. Are you ready?"

She nodded and reached behind her for her zipper.

"Let me," he said and turned her so that her

back was to him. He lowered her zipper all the way down her back to where it ended near the swell of her buttocks. He parted the fabric and gently pushed it from her shoulders. The dress floated to the floor.

He slipped one bra strap over her shoulder and pressed his lips to her skin there. Then he pushed the other strap off her shoulder and kissed her there.

Her breaths became rapid and erratic.

When he flicked the hook on her bra, she clasped the front of the bra to her breasts.

Smoke stopped with his knuckles still brushing against her naked back and waited to see what she would do. He worried he was moving too fast.

Then she lowered the bra, letting it drop to the floor. She stood in nothing but a thin scrap of lacy panties and the shoes she'd worn when she'd kicked a man out the window of the SUV.

Sweet Jesus, she was sexy, her body toned, her muscles firm and her skin soft and silky to the touch. He laid his hands on her hips, giving her time to get used to them on her.

She raised her hands to cover his and then guided them up to cup her breasts. Danny leaned her head back against his chest. "Too slow," she whispered.

"I don't want to spook you," he said against her

ear, while he pinched her nipples gently between his thumbs and forefingers.

Danny moaned. "My body is on fire. How can you go so slowly? I want more. Faster."

He chuckled. "Can we take this to the bedroom?"

"Please," she said, the word coming out on a rush of air.

He scooped her up in his arms. "Which way?"

She tipped her chin toward a half-closed door. "There. Hurry." Wrapping an arm around his neck, she leaned close and pressed her lips to his skin, touching her tongue to the base of his throat where his pulse pounded hard.

He marched toward the door, nudged it open with his foot and carried her to the bed, laying her across the comforter. When he straightened, he reached into his back pocket, pulled out his wallet and extracted the protection he always kept on hand. He laid it on the pillow beside her and brushed a quick kiss across her lips. When she reached for him, he stepped back and smiled, admiring her body lying against a dark gray comforter. Her pale skin glowed in the soft light from the lamp on the nightstand.

"You're beautiful," he said.

"You're still dressed," she noted.

"Not for long." Smoke kicked off his shoes, shucked his jeans and stood before her, his cock jutting out proudly, his body tight with his effort to control the pace, and his growing desire. Then he laid down beside her, gathered her into his arms and kissed her, making love to her mouth before moving on to the rest of her body.

He abandoned her mouth, trailing his lips down the length of her neck and across her collarbone, working his way down to the rounded globes of her pert breasts. Her nipples puckered automatically before he even took one into his mouth. He tapped the tip and rolled it between his teeth until she writhed beneath him. Then he moved to the other breast and gave it similar attention. When he'd had his fill, he kissed a path down her torso, touching every rib, dipping into her belly button with his tongue and diving even lower until he reached the elastic band of her panties.

Hooking the garment with his fingers, he dragged it down her legs and over her ankles, tossing it across the room. Smoke brushed his fingers against the sensitive area behind her knee and skimmed along her inner thigh all the way up to the wedge of curls covering her sex.

"Tell me to stop, and I will," he said.

"Don't. Stop," she cried. "Please." She raised her knees and let them fall to the sides. "This feels so good. So right. I never thought it could be like this."

"Oh, honey, we've only just begun."

. . .

HOW COULD it get better than all the sensations she was already experiencing? Danny reached for Smoke, wanting to feel his skin, to touch his body, to give to him what he was giving her.

He dodged her hand, settled his big body between her thighs and draped her legs over his shoulders. With his thumbs, he parted her folds and blew a stream of air over her heated flesh. He lowered his head and flicked that little nubbin of flesh with the tip of his tongue, sending fireworks bursting through her body.

Danny arched her back and raised her hips, offering herself up to him, urging him to do that magic again.

When he did, she dug her heels into the mattress and bucked beneath him. "Yes," she cried. "There."

He flicked her again and sucked that knot of flesh into his mouth, rolling it around on his tongue.

"Oh, sweet heaven. So good," she moaned. "So good."

He settled into a rhythm of flicking and licking, ratcheting up the tension in her body. When she thought it couldn't get tighter, he slipped two fingers into her channel and swirled them around at the same time as he twisted his tongue around her clit.

Danny's insides exploded in wave after wave of electrical pulses, tingling all the way from her core out to the very tips of her fingers and toes. She rode the waves all the way to the end, collapsing into the mattress, breathless, sated, but not.

Her core ached for more. Her channel wept with her juices. She wanted him inside her.

Now.

She leaned up, gripped his arms and dragged him up her body.

He laughed and surrendered to her guidance, climbing up to settle his hips between her thighs. He bent to claim her lips, tasting of her sex.

She leaned into the kiss and gave as good as she got. When they were forced to breathe again, Smoke rose to his knees, grabbed the packet from the pillow beside her and tore it open.

Danny snagged the condom from his fingers and rolled it down over his engorged cock, wondering how something that long and thick would fit inside her.

Gripping his hips, she drew in a deep breath and guided him to her center, praying she wouldn't flip her shit when he entered her.

Smoke touched the tip of his cock to her entrance. "We can still stop. Your call."

"No. I have to do this," she said.

He shook his head, withdrawing a bit. "You

don't have to do anything. In fact, we should stop here."

"No!" she cried, her fingers tightening on his hips. "I need you. I need to know what it feels like when I want it."

Still, he hesitated. "I don't want to hurt you," he said.

"You're hurting me by holding back."

"Then we'll take it slowly."

She didn't want it slow. Danny wanted him inside her, the sooner the better.

With her fingers curled around his hips, she tightened her hold and pulled him into her.

He dipped the tip of his shaft into her slick entrance and retracted. Pressed a little deeper and came out again.

Beyond her ability to wait another minute, Danny held tightly to Smokes' ass and slammed him home.

She thought she might have flashbacks of her rape if she ever made love with a man, but this was so different and amazing, it was nothing like what had happened to her before.

Smoke buried himself to the hilt and paused to give her channel time to adjust to his length and girth. Then he moved in and out. Slowly at first, and then faster and faster, until he was pumping in and out of her like a piston in a car engine.

This was what she'd been waiting for. The

culmination, the pinnacle. He filled the empty space that had ached for the right touch. His touch. She shot over the edge, the same electric shocks, rippling through her system.

Smoke's body tensed beneath her fingertips. He thrust once more, deep and true, staying the course as his shaft pulsed inside her channel.

They clung to each other through the final shudder.

Smoke collapsed onto Danny and rolled them both to their sides. He lay for a long moment, holding her close, skin to skin, his heat surrounding her.

"Wow," she said with a laugh. "So, that's an orgasm."

"Yes, ma'am," he said with a chuckle.

"I never knew what I was missing," she said. "When can we do that again?"

Smoke laughed out loud. "Woman, you amaze me."

"I'm glad I do. But you didn't answer my question." She leaned up on one elbow and cocked an eyebrow.

"Give me a few minutes to recover," he said. "Hell, I've created a monster."

"Do you need to eat to replenish your reserves?"

His stomach rumbled. "That might help."

Danny rolled out of the bed and padded naked to the table, grabbed their food and returned.

"Aren't you afraid we'll get crumbs in your bed?" he asked, taking the ham sandwich from her hand.

"I don't care. Eat up. The night is short. I don't want to miss a thing." She bit into her sandwich, determined to keep up her strength. Though there had been moments she thought she might lose it, she'd made it past the first test of her ultimate recovery. She'd made love with a man and had had her first honest-to-goodness, mind-blowing orgasm. Not only one... but two.

Along with the realization she could move on with her life after being victimized was the awareness that this man had been the one to inspire her, to dare her to live exceptionally.

She wasn't sure if they had a future together or not, but she'd be forever grateful for his patience and understanding—and his incredible love-making skills. He'd be a tough act to follow.

Danny wasn't sure she wanted any other act, not when this one had proven himself.

CHAPTER 8

SMOKE WOKE to the flutter of a butterfly kiss tickling his lips. He blinked his eyes open and smiled up at Danny, leaning over him.

"Hey," she said.

"Hey." He stretched his arms above his head, cracking the kinks out of his back before settling his arms around Danny's waist. "Ready for a workout?"

"I am," she said and kissed his lips, sliding her mouth over his beard-roughened chin and down his neck. "But not the kind of workout you're thinking."

"Oh, I'm pretty sure we're on the same page," he said.

"Hmm. I can see I need to be a little less transparent. A man loves a woman of mystery, or so the tabloids say."

"I prefer a woman who's straight with me and doesn't play games."

"Then I'm your gal. I wouldn't know how to play a game if I tried." She leaned back. "What you see is what you get."

His gaze swept over her nakedness, his body instinctively reacting, his cock already stiff and eager. But he didn't take the lead this time. He was content to let her explore and experiment on her own.

Danny blazed a path across his chest from one small brown nipple to the other, flicking each with the tip of her tongue. She slid down his torso, her sex gliding across his stiff erection, teasing him, making him insanely tight with need. He'd let her have her way with him, as long as she didn't take all day.

He wouldn't last that long.

Continuing downward, she licked and nipped the skin on his abdomen, angling lower to his jutting staff. She wrapped her hands around him and raised them together, moving up and down, slowly increasing the pace until he couldn't take much more without losing control.

He captured her hands, stilling the motion. "I don't have another condom," he said. "I don't want to risk it."

She smiled. "You don't have to. I understand there are other ways to get there." Danny bent and proceeded to show him which way she had in mind. Once again, she wrapped her hand around his thick cock. Only, this time, she leaned over him and flicked the tip with her tongue.

Smoke tensed. "Much more of that, and I won't be able to hold back."

"Then don't," she said. "This is for you."

"But I like making you happy, too."

"It makes me happy to see you lose it." With a sexy smile, she licked him like an ice cream cone, starting at the base of his shaft and sliding upward to the tip. Once there, she took him into her mouth and lowered her head, taking as much of him as possible until he bumped the back of her throat.

Leaning back, she let him slide out almost all the way before taking him again. She repeated the process, again and again, her mouth warm and wet, and her tongue wonderfully talented.

Danny worked him until his body tensed, and he had to grip her hair to stop her. She glanced up, her lips wet, her eyes smoky with desire.

"I want to be inside you," he said, his voice husky.

"Then be inside me." She climbed up to straddle his hips, lowered herself onto his staff, pausing as his tip nudged her entrance. "You know your body better than I do. Withdraw when you're close. Otherwise, I'm riding this cowboy." She lowered herself onto him, rose on her knees and sank again and again, her breasts bouncing with every move.

Smoke thrust upward, as she came down, driving deeper. He held her hips, guiding her pace as the tension built, roiling upward until he couldn't hold back a moment longer.

He lifted her off him a second before his release.

Danny moved to straddle his thighs, wrapped her hands around his cock and continued to stroke him until he came and fell back against the sheets.

"That ought to be good for a couple dozen squats," Danny said as she climbed off him, took his hand and pulled him from the bed to his feet. "How do you feel about showers?"

"I love them," he said. "Especially if I can share them with someone else."

She grinned and led him into her bathroom.

Thirty minutes later, they emerged from the bathroom, after having made love against the cool tiles and explored every inch of each other's bodies with hands full of soapy suds.

Smoke had never been more invigorated nor felt more alive and ready to face any challenge the day had to offer. All because of one badass woman who was quickly learning how making love could be a beautiful thing when done right. With care and concern for the partner's needs. He hoped he was showing her that not all men were bastards, only concerned about sating their own desires at the expense of whatever women they forcibly raped.

He still burned with anger over what Danny had endured at the hands of one of her fellow countrymen.

Despite making love twice and showering until the water turned cool, they were up before many of the members of the embassy staff.

"My uncle will likely be sleeping another thirty minutes. We can make our own breakfast or wait until the kitchen staff is ready," Danny suggested.

"I can wait." Smoke pulled on his trousers and polo shirt, grabbed his shoes and belt. "I'm going to change into fresh clothes. How long will it be before you're ready?"

"Five minutes." She stood in her bedroom, a towel wrapped around her as she looked through her closet and finally selected a pair of black slacks with a matching blazer and a light gray, short-sleeved sweater. She turned toward him. "What? I don't usually wear makeup, and I only comb the tangles out of my hair and leave it to dry straight. Is that a bad thing? I told you…what you see is what you get."

"I like what I see," he said with a grin. "You're amazing just the way you are."

Her cheeks filled with color. "You're not so bad yourself." She tipped her chin. "Now, go so that I can get ready. There are some things I want to do today."

"There are some things I'd like to do as well." Smoke waggled his eyebrows.

"And we will. Later. I want to do some research for my uncle." She waved him toward the door. "I'll fill you in when we're downstairs in my uncle's office suite and I have access to a computer and the internet."

"Five minutes," he said and headed for the door.

"Four, now," she countered.

"I'll make it three if I don't have to shave," he said with a wink.

"Four. With a shave." She rubbed the side of her cheek. "I have beard burn in more places than I ever imagined." Her smile tempered her words.

"Five minutes and a shave." He left her in her room and hurried to his. After a quick shave using his electric razor, he changed into clean clothes, slapped on some aftershave and stepped out of his apartment into the hallway at the same time Danny emerged.

"Perfect timing," he said.

"My uncle went down a few minutes ago. He called to let me know he was going to grab something quick and head to his office."

"Is he at all concerned about the security here at the embassy?"

"By that, do you mean is he worried someone might attack him from inside the compound?"

Smoke nodded.

"The US employees go through a strict vetting process to join the US Foreign Service."

"What about the Israeli employees?" he asked, having noticed several speaking a different language among the kitchen, housekeeping and waitstaff.

"They go through a strict interview and background check. We've never had problems." Her lips twisted. "Still, I don't like leaving him without coverage for too long."

"I can get my guys to stand guard in shifts if things heat up," Smoke offered.

Danny nodded. "Thanks. I hope it doesn't come to that."

Together, they descended one level and made their way to the dining room, where members of the embassy staff were helping themselves to a breakfast buffet.

Ambassador Turner was just leaving, carrying a cup of coffee. "I have a lot to do today," he said.

"Anything requiring you to leave the embassy?" Danny asked, not having checked the day's schedule, having been preoccupied with one talented Delta.

"Not until later this evening. We have a private meet-and-greet to attend as part of the Invest in

Israel convention going on today and tomorrow. Many of the biggest investors in the Israeli economy will be in attendance, as well as most of the government's leadership, including the Prime Minister, the Minister of Economy and Industry, the Minister of Foreign Affairs and the Ministry of Public Security. To name a few."

"That should make for an interesting evening," Danny said. "Do I need to make sure Asher is on the invitation list?"

"No, dear." Her uncle patted her arm. "My secretary has taken care of it. He'll be on the list to get in. Unfortunately, only you and Smoke will be allowed to accompany me inside. I would like to have at least four other Deltas, one on each exterior corner of the convention center, in case there are any problems. I've already notified them of the detail." The ambassador's gaze slipped over Smoke. "You'll need a suit for the event."

"How formal?" he asked.

"Black suit and bowtie. And while you're at it, rent a tux for tomorrow night. We're to attend a gala at the Waldorf. I'll want the full team for that event. They've hired security, but there will be more people attending that event."

"Will they have metal detectors at the entrances?" Smoke asked.

The ambassador nodded.

Danny frowned. "Do you have to go?"

Her uncle smiled. "It's part of my job to represent our country at these events. We're here to encourage peace and prosperity, protect our citizens and advance our nation's interests abroad. I can't facilitate that undertaking by hiding out in the embassy."

"Not if your life is in danger," Danny argued.

"It won't be just my life. Hundreds of others will be there. They aren't going to stay home because they're afraid. This is a huge opportunity to network and work with investors who might be interested in establishing ties with the US." He lifted his chin. "I'll be there. You two don't have to come."

"We'll be there." Danny's shoulders squared, the fighter in her shining through.

Smoke's heart swelled. She was a Valkyrie from a different time. Tough as nails on the outside and vulnerable on the inside.

The ambassador left them to their breakfast.

They loaded their plates with ham and eggs.

Smoke chuckled when he speared a slice of ham. "You know we never did eat our sandwiches last night."

"Why do you think I'm filling my plate?" Her lips curled into a soft smile. "No regrets on missing a meal."

"Me either," he said.

The large dining table configuration had been

split into smaller tables. Smoke and Danny chose a table in the corner away from the others and ate quickly.

"What is it you want to research for your uncle?" Smoke asked.

"I want to know who provides the supply shipments to the Palestinians in West Bank and who built the settlements the Israeli Jews are living in. I also want to know who sent the shipment of medical supplies and arms to Gaza that got waylaid by the Israeli Navy."

"Do you think they're connected?"

"I don't know. It would help to know who is behind some of the problems. After all, knowledge is power. You can't fix something if you don't know why it's broken." Danny set down her fork and glanced across the table at the man she'd now made love to more times than she'd ever thought possible. "At the very least, we can brief my uncle with that information and let him make the call."

After they finished their meal, they each took a coffee to go and carried them to her uncle's suite of offices. "I'm using one of the advisor's offices. It's this way." She led him into a small office with two wooden desks that had seen much better days. Each desk had a computer and a monitor.

"We can use the Wi-Fi," Danny said. "We just can't bump around in the secret files. Top secret files are protected. You shouldn't be able to access them."

He nodded and pulled up a chair in front of one of the computer monitors and hit the On switch.

The machine's fan whirred to life; the monitor blinked and then filled with a background photo of an island beach. A minute later, Smoke was on the internet, sending a message to a friend with a friend who was a master at "researching" companies with nefarious reputations and tracing them back to the parent corporations that controlled them.

"Do you know where we can get a guest list for tonight and tomorrow night's events?" Smoke asked.

"No, but I know someone who would know." Danny left the room and returned minutes later with the two lists Smoke had requested. "My uncle's secretary is amazing. She can find practically anything. Which one do you want first?"

"I'd like tonight's list," he said. "What are you starting with?"

She handed him the shorter list. "I want to dig around for information about the Jewish settlements encroaching on the Palestinian territories. It might help to know who builds these massive communities and whether they will be in attendance tonight or tomorrow night. I'd like to ask them about their permits—who grants them and how do they get around the treaties governing who the land's rightful owners are."

"Sounds like work." He tipped his head toward the other computer. "You'd better get cracking."

Smoke searched the internet for information about each of the guests attending the next two nights' functions. The more he knew about them, the better prepared he'd be to carry on a conversation. And the better he'd be able to identify any potential threats to the ambassador and his niece.

Several names stood out on the short list for the exclusive party that night.

The prime minister would be an interesting character. He'd publicly announced he supported the idea that Israel should take full control of the lands identified as under the control of the Palestinian Authority. Also, a supporter of the Israeli settlements, he would be a good one to question about the settlements and the poor material quality. Since he'd taken over from the last Israeli leader, relations between the Palestinians and Israelis hadn't improved.

"Is a Benjamin Cohen on tonight's list?" Danny asked from across the room.

Smoke ran his finger over the names and stopped. "Yes, he is." He hadn't gotten to that one yet. "Why?"

"Says on one of the settlement's websites that

Benjamin Cohen is one of the investors in the settlements."

Smoke searched for Cohen's name on the internet and found numerous stories and images. "It appears Mr. Cohen is a billionaire who likes accumulating wealth," Smoke said.

"No kidding. He's built several settlements, shopping centers and service stations. He's also a major stakeholder in Democratic Republic of Congo diamond mines," Danny added. "There's controversy about how he became a major stakeholder. However he did it, his organization owns a number of other organizations. I bet there are even more beneath those." Smoke glanced across at Danny. "We might want to have a conversation with him tonight."

"Definitely," Danny said. "Based on the photographs, he's friends with the new Prime Minister."

"Which means more encroaching settlements into the Palestinian Territories." Smoke shook his head. "I get the feeling Cohen thrives on chaos. The worse things are, the more he sells."

"Nothing like taking advantage of bad situations," Danny said. "A vulture looking for easy pickings."

They spent the next hour in silence.

Smoke found an article about the Minister of Economy and Industry, Gideon Horowitz, stating a company in which he held stock had been involved in an insider trading deal, based on information only he could have known via his position in the government. His name had been cleared when he'd claimed he no longer owned stock in that company, having sold it prior to the company making the deal. Smoke suspected the man had sold it to another company buried in a maze of holdings designed to hide the owners' identities.

He sent the Minister's name to his friend to have his friend dig up dirt on him as well. Then he forwarded Benjamin Cohen's name, asking if he had other connections they should be concerned about besides the apparent ownership of the corporation funding the settlements. By the time lunch rolled around, Smoke was deep into the list of guests.

"Are you hungry?" Danny asked.

He shook his head. "Not really. Do you want me to go down with you?"

She smiled. "Of course. But I see that you're busy and my uncle is also buried in work. I'm going down to fix sandwiches. Want me to bring one back for you?"

At the mention of sandwiches, his attention shot up to Danny, his pulse kicking up a notch. For the rest of his life, sandwiches would bring back a lot of different memories from those of picnics and school lunches. He'd think of sitting naked in bed with Danny while their sandwiches remained on the table where it had all started.

"Just sandwiches," Danny said with a laugh.

"You went there too, didn't you?" He stood, pulled her into his arms and kissed her soundly.

She rested her hand on his chest and stared up into his eyes. "As soon as I said the word, I was there in my apartment with you in my bed. Hungry, but full."

"Save some energy for tonight," he whispered against her ear. "We'll make more sandwiches after the event."

She chuckled all the way out of the room.

Smoke dropped back into his seat and went to work on the name he'd been researching. When it came up unimpressive, he pushed back from his seat. When Danny had been in the room, he'd been content to stay. Her absence made him want to find her, to be with her and hear her laughter, see her smile and smell the fragrance of her shampoo in her sandy-blond hair.

He stretched for a moment and decided to join her in the kitchen to help her make…sandwiches. With a smile on his face, he checked in with Ambassador Turner's secretary. "Is the ambassador in?"

She nodded. "He's committing death by documents."

Smoke grinned. "Would he mind if I popped in?"

"I'm sure he could use a break." She tipped her head toward the door.

Smoke knocked lightly at the ambassador's door.

"Enter," called out a muffled voice.

Smoke pushed open the door and ducked his head inside. "Ambassador Turner, are you surviving?"

The man shoved a hand through his shock of white hair. "If you call this surviving." He waved at the stacks of folders on his desk. "I thought we were heading for a paperless society." He sighed. "What happened to that concept?"

"It's not fully implemented, like electric cars."

The ambassador waved his hand. "Please, come in, Mr. Gray, and have a seat. My niece has gone to fetch sandwiches. She should be back soon."

Smoke nodded. "I know. I was considering joining her to see if she could use some help."

"The kitchen staff will have her fixed up in no time. She'll be back before you can get up to the kitchen to help. Besides, I wanted to spend some time with my niece's fiancé." He smiled at the word. "How's it going with your *engagement*?"

"Fine, sir. Your niece is a beautiful, intelligent woman."

"Yes, yes, she is." He nodded. "You two seem to be getting along rather well."

"Yes, sir. I think highly of Danica," Smoke said, his brow furrowing. Where was the ambassador going with this conversation?

"That's good. I think highly of her, too, and would hate to see her hurt in any way." Turner rose from his office chair and paced across the room and back. "The threats have increased against me. I get them in my emails, through the post and the graffiti painted on the outer walls of the embassy. Some of the messages wish death on the Americans and the ambassador."

"I'm sorry to hear that," Smoke said. "Do you not feel safe within the walls of this compound?"

"It's not just the walls of the compound." Ambassador Turner faced Smoke. "I want you to promise me that if anything happens to me, you'll make certain my niece gets back to the States safely."

Smoke nodded, his brow furrowing. "Yes, sir. I promise."

"And if anything happens to my Danny, you'll do everything in your power to save her, even if it means leaving me."

"Sir, I'd risk my life to see to your niece's safety." His frown deepening, Smoke stared at the older man. "Is there something you're not telling us?"

The ambassador glanced away, his gaze going to the window. "The threats aren't targeted at just me. They're threatening my family as well. Specifically, my niece."

"Why?"

"The people sending the anonymous threats accuse the US of denying their children the medical supplies they need. If one child dies because they didn't receive the supplies that were on the confiscated ship, they will make the Americans suffer as they have. An eye for an eye. Or, in this case, a loved one for a loved one."

Smoke's gut clenched. "Sir, I promise I'd give my last breath to save Danny from harm."

Ambassador Turner met his gaze, holding it for a long time before he nodded. "Thank you. If I could talk her into going back to the States, I would."

Smoke chuckled. "But she's hardheaded and loyal to the ones she loves."

Turner nodded. "She wouldn't leave me here. She's assigned herself as my personal bodyguard whether I want her to do that or not."

A smile played at the corners of Smoke's lips. "And she wasn't too happy about having a backup."

The ambassador shared a smile with him. "I'm glad you and your team are here. I have a feeling things will get worse before they get better."

"We'll do our best to keep you and your niece safe," Smoke said.

"Hey, what's the big deal?" Danny's voice sounded from the doorway. "I leave for a few minutes, and you two get together sharing secrets. No fair." Her eyebrows formed a V over her nose. "I'll trade you a roast beef sandwich for your secrets." She held up two clear plastic bags with sandwiches inside. "Well?"

Smoke shot a glance at the ambassador. "If we told you our secrets, we'd have to kill you."

"YOU'D HAVE to catch me first," she said. "Fine. I'd hold out on the food, but my daddy taught me not to waste. I don't like it when you don't tell me what's going on."

"We were just talking about the ship, the medical supplies and the people who are angry because they didn't get their stuff," Smoke said. "Is that one for me?" he asked, reaching for the bag dangling from her fingertips.

"No," she said. "That's for the ambassador. He has to keep up his strength for the evening. That event is likely to last past his bedtime of nine o'clock."

"I stay up later than nine-thirty," her uncle said.

"Okay, nine-thirty-five," she offered, a smile

pulling at her lips. "To tell the truth, I like going to bed before nine. Does that make me old?"

Smoke and the ambassador answered as one, "Yes." And they laughed.

Danny's lips twisted. "I see how it is. The two guys gang up on the lone female to poke fun at her." She nodded. "Uh-huh. Jerks." She handed her uncle his sandwich and Smoke his. Then she took hers out of the plastic bag and bit into the roast beef sandwich.

Smoke couldn't wipe the smile off his face as he ate his sandwich in the ambassador's office, staring at the man's niece, the woman with whom he'd spent the night before, making hot, sexy love into the wee hours of the morning.

The assignment to provide support and security to the ambassador and his niece had graduated from an annoying task, that had promised to be boring, to holy shit, this could be the most complicated job he'd ever taken on. The most complicating factor being his feelings for the woman he'd sworn to protect. Hell, was he falling in love with her? He schooled his face to poker straight as he studied the woman in question for a long moment. Was it possible that she was even more beautiful today in her black pantsuit than she'd been in the shiny blue dress she'd worn when she'd knocked him on his ass? The pantsuit made her look even more sophisticated and capable.

His heart swelled inside his chest. He did have feelings for the young woman and could be well on the way to falling in love with her, something he'd sworn he'd never do while married to the Army.

Man, he was screwed.

CHAPTER 9

DANNY CHECKED her reflection for the hundredth time, looked at the numbers on her digital clock and huffed a sigh. Why the hell did she have to be so punctual, to the point she was painfully early for every event? She checked the clock again. They were leaving in five minutes. The vehicles would be waiting outside the building. If she left her room now, would she appear too eager to the point of being needy? Why did being a woman have to be so hard? She could use a book of the rules women had to follow while dating.

The alternative was to wait in her apartment for Smoke to knock on her door. She'd walk slowly across the floor in her insanely high heels, fling open the door and mesmerize him with the sexy, slinky black dress that fit her body like a glove. God, she hoped her breasts didn't slip out of the sides of the barely-there bodice. She must have been insane for letting the clerk choose the dress for her. Then again, she had no clue how to wear dresses. She'd been a tomboy all her life. The Army and MMA hadn't improved her femininity.

Guys liked women who acted like women, not like other men.

Her shoulders sagged. She'd told Smoke the truth. What he saw was what he got. She couldn't be anyone but herself, whether she was dressed in camouflage or a skin-tight dress and high heels she was sure she'd break an ankle wearing. The girl inside the clothes was the same awkward human who would kick the ass of anyone who tried to mess with her.

She started back to her bedroom to find a different outfit. Maybe sweats or workout leggings. Or maybe, she just wouldn't go to the event. Smoke could handle looking out for her uncle.

As she passed the door to her apartment, a knock sounded, making her jump and teeter on her heels. She grabbed the back of her sofa to steady herself. Her heart pounding, she hurried for the door. When she reached it, she stopped, took a breath and plumped her breasts for courage. Though her pulse still raced, she schooled her face to be the image of calm then twisted the handle, opening the door like a lady. At least how she thought a lady should. What did she know? Her father had taught her to hunt and fish, not to flirt and walk like a model down a runway.

Her gaze met Smoke's, and her nerves abated a little. His deep gray eyes flashed as they swept her from head to toe. "Wow," he said. "Just wow."

"Is it too much?" she asked. "Or should I say too little?"

He shook his head. "It's absolutely perfect. You're going to make every woman wish she was you and every man wish he was me."

Her cheeks warmed. "Thank you. I feel like a little girl playing dress-up or like my coach will turn into a pumpkin at midnight."

"No way," Smoke said. "You're the real thing. The magic is purely you."

Her knees shook at the words, and tears blurred her vision. She'd never had a man say things like that. It made her warm all over and glad she'd worn the dress, no matter how uncomfortable.

Smoke took her hand and lifted it to his lips, pressing a kiss to the backs of her knuckles. "Are you ready?"

She was ready to step back into her apartment with him, lock the door and not come out until the morning. Maybe until the following week. Instead, she nodded.

"Your uncle is in the foyer with the members of my team who will accompany us to the event venue."

"In other words, I'm the one holding them up?" Her cheeks burned. "I'm never late." She hurried toward the stairs.

Smoke slipped an arm around her waist and blocked her from turning. "We'll take the elevator. I don't trust those heels on the stairs."

"Oh. Right." She walked with him to the elevator and stepped inside, glad he'd had the foresight to know she might not have made it down two flights without falling or twisting an ankle. Her night would end before it began, and she'd be of no use to her uncle, laid up with a broken bone.

She faced him as the elevator car descended to the ground floor. "You look amazing in that suit."

He dipped his head. "Thank you. I can clean up sometimes. And a good thing. I couldn't show up in desert camouflage to escort the prettiest girl."

The door slid open.

Danny's uncle stood near the front entrance with five men, dressed in black trousers and black, long-sleeve shirts. They were well-dressed, but not in a suit like Smoke.

When they spotted Danny and Smoke, the men's eyes rounded and smiles spread across their faces.

"Damn, Smoke, where did you get the suit? I know you didn't have that hidden in the bottom of your go bag," Gonzo said.

"I rented it," Smoke said.

Danny joined her uncle, reaching up to adjust the man's bowtie. "You really did need Aunt Ruth, didn't you?"

Her uncle nodded. "I'm lost without her when it comes to tying ties and planning dinner parties."

"I can handle the ties." Danny patted her uncle's chest and stepped back. "Daddy taught me how. As for dinner parties...I wouldn't know a salad fork from a dessert fork."

"You look amazing," her uncle said.

"Yes, she does," Ketch said.

Danny smiled at the Delta. "Thank you."

Rome walked all the way around Smoke, stopped and shook his head. "Man, you clean up well."

Voodoo took in a deep breath. "He even smells good. But his date outshines him by a million watts." He turned to Smoke. "I'd give my eyeteeth to trade places with you tonight."

"Keep your teeth. You might need them." Smoke rested a hand at the small of Danny's back. "Sorry, guys. Danny is *my* fiancée. I'm a little territorial when it comes to her."

Danny's heart swelled. She knew it was all an act for anyone who might be listening, but it felt good to have his hand on her back and his protection.

"We can understand why." Ice reached for Danny's hand and stared into her eyes. "When you wise up and realize you're with the wrong man, I'll be waiting."

Smoke punched the man in the arm. "Back off."

The gesture appeared playful, but Ice flinched and rubbed the spot.

They loaded into shiny black SUVs, the five men in the lead vehicle, Smoke, Danny and her uncle in the second.

Danny sat between the two men as the driver wove through the streets of Jerusalem to the hotel where the event would take place.

The lead SUV drove past the hotel and stopped a block away. The men exited the vehicle and walked casually back to the hotel.

"They'll take up positions at the corners where they can observe the entrances on all sides," Smoke whispered into her ear.

She liked that the Deltas were there in case they needed them. "How will you communicate?" she asked.

Smoke touched a transparent earbud seated in his left ear.

Danny grinned. "Next time, I want one."

Smoke nodded. "Done." He slipped out of the SUV and offered her his hand to help her down.

Once she was safely on the ground, they walked into the building and through a metal detector. Once inside, a hotel employee directed them to an escalator that took them to the second level and a small ballroom with massive crystal chandeliers.

Standing at the entry to the ballroom were the Israeli Prime Minister, his wife, the Minister of Economy and Industry, Gideon Horowitz, and several other Ministers Danny recognized from her research that day.

She greeted each with a smile and a firm handshake. Once past the reception line, she glanced around, searching the faces for the people she wanted to speak with, mainly Benjamin Cohen. She'd corner the Minister of Economy and Industry later.

"Can I get you a drink?" Smoke asked.

Danny nodded. "Whiskey, neat."

He chuckled. "I should've figured that."

She shrugged. "My father raised me. He preferred his whiskey pure. No ice, not chilled. Straight out of the bottle into a glass. I'm my father's daughter."

"Where is he now?" Smoke asked.

"In Michigan, where we grew up," the ambassador answered. "Probably fishing. Like I should be."

"You're performing a vital national function," Danny said. "If you only knew how proud my dad is of his big brother. He tells anyone who'll listen about his brother who works in the Foreign Service." She smiled. "He always wished he could've served his full twenty in the Marine Corps. If he hadn't blown out his knee, he would have."

"It was a terrible shame. Dan wanted to be a Marine from the moment he understood what being one meant. He was the most athletic, the strongest, fastest and most coordinated of us. It was his dream to serve his country. It must've broken his heart when they medically boarded him out after only six years."

Danny nodded. "I was five at the time. I remember moving back to Michigan with Mom and Dad. It was a sad time. Dad was on crutches. He couldn't put weight on his leg. Mom had to do most of the unpacking. I was too little to help much. I just remember Dad being so very sad. Mom worked hard to make the house a home and to bring Dad out of his depression. Once he healed enough, he got a job with the US post office. He's been with them ever since."

"Are he and your mother still together?" Smoke asked.

"Sadly no," Danny said. "My mother died of cancer six years later. That's why my father raised me. I was eleven. We only had each other. Dad did the best he could."

"He did good," Smoke said. "He taught you how to drink whiskey."

Uncle James laughed. "Daniel is a good man. I

need to make a trip back to Michigan. It's been a long time."

"Yes, you do," Danny said. "Dad would love that."

"Ambassador Turner, what would you like to drink?" Smoke asked.

"I'll stick with water," he said. "Israel allows people to drink alcohol, but the dominant religions forbid the consumption of alcohol. I find it easier not to offend people by abstaining until I'm in the privacy of my quarters."

"Would you rather we did the same?" Danny asked.

Her uncle shook his head. "Not at all." He lifted his chin toward other guests in the room. "If you'll notice, at least half the guests are drinking alcoholic beverages. It's okay." He looked across the room, his eyebrows rising. "If you'll excuse me, the receiving line is disbanding. I want to catch the Prime Minister before he's swarmed."

Danny touched her uncle's arm as he turned away. "Do you want me to come?"

He shook his head. "That won't be necessary. As long as you two are in the same room, I'm sure I'll be fine." Her uncle left her in the middle of the floor.

"Come with me to get that drink," Smoke urged.

She shook her head. "I'm in a good position to

see who's coming through the door and who is already in the ballroom. I'll wait here for you."

His lips pressed into a tight line. "Okay, but remember, you could be a target as well as your uncle. The threats are against the US government. The ambassador represents the US in Israel. You, by default, are also a representative since you're his family."

She smiled. "I'll maintain situational awareness at all times. Now, go get me that whiskey before I'm too old to drink it."

"Mouthy woman," Smoke muttered, a hint of a smile on his lips.

Danny cocked an eyebrow. "Bossy man."

He walked away, muttering beneath his breath something about never winning with females.

Danny chuckled as she watched Smoke walk toward the bar. The man probably had no idea just how sexy he was. Even his walk had the swagger of a man who was confident in his own skin.

She counted the minutes until she could see him in nothing but his own skin later that night.

"Ms. Turner, I presume?" an accented voice sounded from behind Danny.

She turned, pasting a smile on her face, and discovered the one person she wanted to speak with most. Benjamin Cohen.

She recognized his dark, slightly unkempt hair and thick, brown beard. The man had just turned forty and was already a billionaire. He had been for several years. He obviously knew how to form alliances with influential people and how to turn a profit, no matter what business. He was known to be ruthless and an asshole, but he got the job done, even if it meant breaking a few laws along the way. The man wore a permanent sneer, one side of his mouth lifting in a half-smile that didn't appear friendly at all.

Despite her instant aversion to the man, Danny pasted a smile on her own face and held out her hand. "Mr. Cohen," she said. "Just the person I wanted to see."

He took her hand in his and held it longer than was necessary or appropriate. "I'm flattered," he said, his accent more British English than anything else she could detect.

She'd read that his mother had moved from Jerusalem to London when he'd been a boy, raising him as a British citizen until he was a teenager. She'd met and married a fellow Jew when Benjamin was thirteen and moved him back to Israel, where he'd worked part-time in his step-father's diamond business. A smart kid, he'd skipped a couple of levels in his education and had gone to college at the tender age of fifteen, graduating with a degree in finance. He'd started investing his stepfather's money, and then his own, until he'd amassed a sizable sum and invested in planned communities, the beginning of the settlements.

"My uncle, the US ambassador, my fiancé and I had the pleasure of visiting one of the planned communities you helped build. I'm intrigued."

His smile took root on both sides of his mouth briefly. "Do you have questions?"

She nodded. "How did you get involved in such a large undertaking? I mean, you didn't just create homes, you created much of the infrastructure for the small town."

He nodded. "With the influx of people moving to Israel, prices on existing homes climbed. People needed a lot of affordable housing fast. To build homes quickly, we chose to place them further away from cities with heavy traffic. The land was less expensive and available in larger tracts. We purchased several hundred acres in various locations. The problem with large communities in out-of-the-way places is the lack of infrastructure. We solved that by incorporating that infrastructure into the planning process."

"It's impressive what can be done with the right idea and a lot of money." Danny's brow dipped. "With the amount of building that goes into such a large undertaking, I'm surprised you were able to keep the supplies flowing. Who did you go to for lumber, concrete, plumbing and more?"

Cohen puffed out his chest and lifted his chin.

"As you know, Israel is not a land-rich country. We have a limited number of natural resources. We must rely on other countries for those resources. I was able to obtain all the resources I needed by making our project the number one priority to complete."

"Have you experienced any issues regarding substandard materials or appliances?" Danny persisted.

Cohen's eyes narrowed. "Is there a reason for your interest in my construction projects?

She nodded. "Actually, there is. I spoke with some of the people living in one of your planned communities. For the most part, they're happy with the concept and glad to have homes." Danny's forehead creased. "Many of them have issues with plumbing, appliances, and with windows that weren't installed correctly or were flawed before installation. What is your organization doing to address the problems?"

The man's forehead creased. "They purchased their homes. They are now the owners and responsible for maintaining them."

"Even if they were built with substandard materials?" she asked, her voice lowering. "Could you not go back to your suppliers and demand that they make it right?"

The man stared at her with narrowed eyes. "Ms.

Turner, you are in a country that is not your own. Who are you to question your host?"

"I read that most supplies, whether for building or basic needs like food and medicine, are hard to come by and are expensive. The Palestinians in the West Bank are being given substandard supplies like second-class citizens and not enough when they need it."

"Why is this my concern?" Cohen said. "I do not live in the West Bank."

"No, but I looked. Your corporation owns the warehouses that supply those people. I'm guessing you also determine what goes into the warehouses and what gets distributed. I suspect if I look long and hard enough, we'll discover your organization supplied all the materials used to construct your settlements. On land you don't own or have a right to build on."

Cohen grabbed her arm and pinched it hard. "An event like this is neither the time nor the place to spread your lies."

She raised her chin, aware that anger was heating up her cheeks. "What better time and place to reveal to potential investors the character of the man you're considering working with. A man who made millions on the settlements which are displacing an entire population. There is never a right time or place to discuss shoddy work, broken promises and the mistreatment of people. Do you have trouble sleeping at night?" She swung her hand up and knocked his hand free of her arm. "Is that how you made your millions—on the backs of those you were paid to help? Are you working small children in one of your African diamond mines?"

He grabbed her arm again and pulled her toward an empty corridor. "You will not talk to me in this manner."

Danny let Cohen lead her out of the main ball-room because she didn't want to cause a stir and embarrass her uncle in front of all the diplomats, politicians and investors who could potentially bring more industry to the Israelis, and maybe even the US. When they were sufficiently out of sight and hearing of the others, Danny planted her high heels against the floor. "Sir, if you do not unhand me, I will be forced to hurt you."

Cohen snorted and refused to relinquish his grip.

"Why do people refuse to see reason?" She stared him in the eye then brought her arms up sharply, easily knocking his hands away. Danny leaped away.

She had barely broken free of Cohen when the crazy billionaire lunged for her, trapping her against the wall.

His use of force triggered all the memories of being held down and raped by a man she should have been able to trust. Burning rage ripped through her.

"Now, you've done it," she said in a low, thick voice.

"Shut up," Cohen said, pressing his forearm against her mouth to quiet her words.

Counting to three, she breathed in, breathed out, and then erupted in a blur of motion, slamming the palm of her hand into his nose.

The man roared and launched himself back at Danny.

Danny dodged him, spun, hiked up her dress and delivered a sideways kick into his belly, sending him flying against a wall. Danny regretted she hadn't kicked him harder, knocking his zealot self out.

Cohen charged her again.

Before he reached her, another figure plowed into him, sending him sliding down the hallway to the end.

For all his money, the billionaire was no competition. He lurched to his feet, snarling. One look at Smoke standing like a bulked-up weight-lifter, and Cohen straightened his blazer and walked right past Smoke and Danny, slipping into the men's restroom.

Smoke gripped Danny's elbow lightly. If she needed to get away, all she had to do was walk. She was still shaking.

"Hey," he said, studying her expression.

She laughed, the sound without humor. "Hey."

"Did that bastard hurt you?"

She shook her head. "No. I had him. I just didn't want to alert the entire event to what was going on."

Smoke chuckled. "I knew you were perfectly capable of taking care of yourself. But thanks for the timing. It gave my ego a much-needed boost."

"Your ego didn't need a boost," she said, slipping her hand through his elbow as they walked back to the ballroom. "It's already overly inflated."

He touched a hand to his chest. "I'm wounded."

"You'll heal." She lifted her chin and stepped out into the ballroom, proud, strong and able to protect herself. And thankful for a little help from a sexy Delta Force Operative.

CHAPTER 10

"THAT WAS BENJAMIN COHEN?" Smoke verified.

Danny smiled at one of the Ministers passing by and nodded. "He's a real piece of work," she said through gritted teeth and a pasted-on smile.

Anger continued to burn through Smoke at Cohen's treatment of Danny. She'd assured him that she'd had everything under control. And she probably had. But the fact the man hadn't backed down and had continued to assault her made Smoke hot, even five minutes later, when he'd had time to cool down.

He kept an eye on the hallway leading to the restrooms but never saw Cohen emerge. He hoped the man had found a way to leave and was now well away from the ballroom and hotel. If he came one step near Danny again, Smoke wouldn't let him walk away this time.

"There you are." Ambassador Turner walked up beside Danny and frowned down at her. "Are you feeling well, my dear?"

"Yes, of course," she managed through tight lips. "Why do you ask?"

"Your cheeks are flushed. Are you sure you aren't feeling feverish?" Her uncle stared into her face, concern creasing his brow.

Danny made a visible effort to give her uncle a softer smile. "I'm fine," she said.

"We don't have to stay the entire length of time. In fact, after I make one more round of the floor, we can leave," he said.

That worked for Smoke. After the incident with Cohen, he had no desire to grin and shake hands with people he didn't know or give a flying flip about. He wanted to take Danny back to the hotel, get naked and hold her close the rest of the night. Seeing her in trouble had brought out every protective gene he'd been born with, and then some. He wanted to hold her close in the safety of his arms and shield her from all the bastards who preyed on women, using their superior strength to force them into submission.

Smoke's gut roiled at how vicious Cohen had been in his attack. The man probably had taken a hit to his masculinity, being bested by a woman.

Well good. Maybe he'd think twice before assaulting another.

Pride for Danny swelled in Smoke's chest. She'd come a long way from the woman who'd been sexually assaulted while on active duty. He wished he could have seen her in the MMA ring. Then again, he wouldn't have been able to stand by and watch her take the hits without wanting to leap into the ring and shield her from her opponent. Thankfully, she'd left that occupation behind for good. The sport was dangerous.

He snorted softly. Not that the US Foreign Service was any less dangerous. The people who represented the US in embassies in other countries put their lives on the line every day. The US didn't always have a golden reputation in other parts of the world. The leaders of his country hadn't always done right by their allies. Sometimes, they made promises they didn't keep. In the case of the captured ship full of medical supplies and arms, the US had been right not to protect it to its destination, and the Israelis had been justified to waylay the shipment and confiscate the arms. However, if at all possible, they should have sent the medical supplies on to Gaza. Perhaps they would have if they hadn't been compromised. The people there needed anything they could get.

Static crackled in Smoke's ear. "How's it going in there?" Ketch's voice came through softly but clearly.

Smoke glanced around to make sure no one was near him.

Danny was quietly speaking with her uncle, her gaze on the Prime Minister and the Minister of Economy and Industry.

"All's well," Smoke said softly. Things hadn't been so great a few minutes before, but between Smoke and Danny, they had it handled.

"I haven't actually gained an audience with the Prime Minister yet," Ambassador Turner said. "It appears he's freeing up. I'm going to try to get in now. Wish me luck."

"Go get 'em, tiger," Danny said and remained with Smoke as her uncle marched across the ballroom floor, stopping in front of the Israeli Prime Minister and his entourage.

"Good. Once he's done with the PM, we can call it a night," Danny murmured. She shot a glance his way. "How are you holding up?"

"Never better," he lied. After his run-in with the bastard of a filthy-rich Israeli, Smoke couldn't relax. His instincts were screaming at him to leave the ballroom, the building and the immediate vicinity surrounding it. He didn't like that Cohen had disappeared. Smoke felt better when he could see the snake in the grass rather than only the grass, knowing a snake was hiding inside.

Hopefully, the jerk had tucked his tail between his legs and crawled back under the rock he belonged under. People like Cohen gave rich people a bad name. From all he'd read about the man, he hadn't treated the people who'd helped him find success very well. The diamond mines in which he was a stakeholder in DRC used child labor. Cohen and his corporations had controlled much of the mining operations in the DRC until a new president had come to power and had exposed the corruption.

Yeah. Danny had called it. The man was a piece of work. And if the news reports were true about the collapse of the man's mining empire in the DRC, Cohen might be scrambling to maintain the lifestyle he had become accustomed to. Sanctions had been levied against him, freezing his bank accounts.

Smoke held out his hand.

Danny slipped hers into his palm and squeezed gently. A moment of peace settled over him for the briefest of moments. As long as he had Danny by his side, all was right with the world.

The crowd of guests shifted, moving about the ballroom floor. A group of more than twenty people crossed between the ambassador and where Danny and Smoke stood.

For a moment, he lost sight of the ambassador.

Danny tensed beside him and craned her neck, searching the sea of faces. "Do you see my uncle?"

Taller than Danny, Smoke should have been able to locate the man. "No."

Danny released his hand. "I'm going in."

"Me, too."

"It might be better to split up and go around this bunch," Danny said. "They're pretty tight. I'll go right."

Smoke went left, circling around the large group taking up the center of the floor. He spotted the Prime Minister and several other ministers but no Ambassador Turner. His gut tightened. He hadn't given up yet. Across the floor, he spotted Danny taking the long way around the other end of the crowd, moving with purpose, her head held high, her gaze sweeping the crowd.

If they didn't find the ambassador in the next minute or two, Smoke would warn the men outside to be on the lookout in case the ambassador had left the hotel on his own volition or under duress.

At that moment, he spotted US Ambassador James Turner speaking with a woman Smoke recognized from one of the images he'd studied earlier that day. He couldn't recall her name, but she was one of the Israeli ministers.

Relief washed over Smoke as he headed for the ambassador, while now searching the ballroom floor for Danny, wishing he'd had the foresight to give her one of the communication devices his team was using.

As he approached Ambassador Turner, the man smiled, nodded and excused himself from the minister and met Smoke in the middle of the ballroom. "Have you come to tell me you and Danny are ready to leave?" he asked, looking around. "Where's Danny?"

"We split up to find you."

"I've been right here. I haven't seen her." He joined Smoke in his search.

"I don't see her," the ambassador said.

Neither did Smoke. He didn't like it. His gut was telling him to find her...and do it quickly.

A door opened at the far end of the ballroom where the four-piece quartet was playing.

A movement caught Smoke's attention in the corner of his eye. As he turned, so too did others, and a collective gasp sounded from those looking in the direction of the string quartet, who, one by one stopped playing.

People in the crowd nudged one another and turned their attention to the small boy who walked out of what appeared to be a sound room behind the stage. A small, ragged boy in the middle of the well-dressed wealthy crowd was enough to draw attention. But what he had wrapped around his body quickly silenced the chatter.

His eyes were wide, dark pools of fear. His feet shuffled, and tears slipped from the corners of his eyes.

"Holy hell," the ambassador whispered. "He's loaded with explosives."

Smoke had already deduced that. It was what was in the boy's hand that made a cold shiver of dread ripple down his spine. The boy held a grenade with the handle clutched in his small hand, the pin missing.

Whispers swelled into urgent words spoken aloud. A member of the hotel staff stepped forward. "Ladies and gentlemen, remain calm and move quickly to the nearest exit. The police have been notified, and a bomb squad is on the way."

Small cries sounded from some of the women as they moved toward the exits. They would have to descend stairs to the ground level before they would reach an exterior door.

The crowd pressed close together, funneling through the ballroom doors on their way to the escalator. The people were so tightly packed that moving against the flow was not an option.

Fortunately, Smoke and the Ambassador were able to work their way to the side of the room, where they waited for the swell of guests to pass.

Smoke looked for the sandy-blond beauty in the sexy black dress to no avail. The river of people swept past, frightened men and women desperate to get as far away from the boy as possible.

Smoke touched the communications device in his ear. "Guys, we have a suicide bomber in the ballroom. Everyone is moving toward the exits. We've lost sight of Danny. Be on the lookout for her as people leave the building."

"Roger," Ketch said. "I heard sirens headed this way and wondered what was happening."

"Dude," Gonzo's voice came through. "Most suicide bombers don't walk in and hang around. And they don't just let people leave."

Smoke stared across the room at the child, his heart pinching hard inside his chest. "I don't think it was his idea. It's a kid, maybe eight or nine years old. He's wearing a vest of explosives and has a grenade in his hand."

"Pin pulled?" Ketch asked.

Smoke nodded. "Yup. Israeli police and bomb squad are on the way. I didn't want to approach the kid until most of the people were evacuated."

"Smoke," Ketch said. "We don't need dead heroes. Let the bomb squad handle him."

The child stood with tears slipping down his cheeks, staring at the grenade held out in front of him. His hand shook.

"I don't think we can wait."

"Are you sure they're evacuating the building?" Ice's voice sounded in Smoke's ear.

Smoke frowned. "Almost everyone is out of the ballroom. They should be outside by now."

Screams sounded from outside the doors of the ballroom.

"Damn," Ketch said. "I can't open the doors. They're chained from the inside."

"I just tried the rear exit," Gonzo said. "No chain here, but the lock is jammed."

Ice, Rome and Voodoo all reported the same.

"Fire trucks and ambulances are arriving now," Ketch said. "I know I said don't be a hero, but…"

"I know," Smoke said. "I can't let the kid drop the grenade." He looked toward the ambassador. "Sir, you need to go down to the main level and get out of the building as soon as they clear the doors."

Ambassador Turner's brow dipped low. "What are you going to do?"

Smoke tipped his head toward the boy. "Keep the boy from dropping the grenade."

"I'm staying with you," the ambassador said.

Smoke shook his head. "I need you to get out of the building, find Danny and make sure she's safe. I don't like this situation."

"And you think I do?" the ambassador looked from the boy to the exit.

"Go, sir," Smoke said in a calm yet insistent tone. "I need to know your niece is safe."

"You should go and let me deal with the grenade."

Smoke shook his head. "I have more experience with explosives. Please, sir. Take care of your niece."

The older man hesitated a moment longer then

touched Smoke's shoulder. "I'll see you outside." He turned and hurried out of the ballroom.

Smoke approached the boy slowly, smiling gently.

The closer he got, the more the boy shook. By now, his entire body trembled.

"It's okay," Smoke said, speaking in a calm, soothing tone. "I'm not going to leave you." He studied the boy carefully. Not only was the pin pulled on the grenade, but a tripwire had been rigged so that if the grenade were removed from his hands, the wire would probably trigger a detonator hidden somewhere inside the vest full of explosives. As much as Smoke wanted to take the grenade out of the boy's hand, he couldn't.

The child's hands shook badly, and his body trembled to the point Smoke was afraid the detonator would go off without the boy dropping the grenade. He did the only thing he could think to do. He sat on the floor behind the boy, pulled him gently into his lap and wrapped his arms around him. Then he cupped his hands around the child's hands and held him steady until the bomb squad could untangle the mess without destroying the hotel, the boy and Smoke.

As MUCH AS Danny wanted to be with Smoke and her uncle, she had no choice but to go with the flow of the crowd, headed for the exit. If she didn't, she'd be pushed to the ground and trampled. One woman fell in front of her. The push from behind didn't allow anyone to stop to help the woman. Danny grabbed the lady's arm and dragged her up between her and the man in front of her. The woman was in tears, her makeup smeared, a gash on her forehead and bruises on her arms. If the bomb went off, she might have been better off being trampled to death.

When the front of the mob reached the exits to find the doors blocked, the people in the rear didn't stop their forward movement. Men and women were so tightly packed together they couldn't breathe.

Danny couldn't breathe, nor could she move her arms. All the physical training in the world couldn't get her out of the trap of humanity she found herself in. She prayed Smoke and her uncle had found another way out. If the doors didn't open soon, folks would suffocate to death.

Minutes passed. The woman beside her sobbed softly. With every breath she took, her lungs had to be compressing more.

The doors jiggled several times as someone on the outside tried to open them. Each time, hope spiked in Danny, only to be dashed. The doors remained closed.

Sirens wailed outside the hotel. Surely the fire

department could break through the doors and get them out of the building. They'd better hurry before people started dying.

Danny's vision blurred. She tried to hold on, to stay awake and survive, but the lack of oxygen was quickly taking its toll on her and the people around her.

The sobbing woman had grown ominously silent.

A loud metal-on-metal sound rent the air, and one set of doors were flung open.

The crowd surged forward again, pushing those in the middle tighter before the mass of humanity in front could squeeze through the one opening. Another door opened, and then another. Soon, people were moving through. When the man in front of Danny inched forward, she greedily sucked in a breath, filling her lungs. Slowly, the fog in her mind cleared.

Minutes passed as the emergency personnel untangled the men and women packed like sardines in the lobby. Some had to be carried out; others were able to walk out on their own.

By the time Danny made it out into the open night air, half an hour had passed since the boy had walked into the ballroom. She spent a few minutes replenishing the oxygen in her lungs and brain cells while searching the faces in the shadows for the ones she wanted to see most. When she didn't see

Smoke or her uncle anywhere among the people moving further away from the building, she worked her way back to where police guarded the door, refusing entrance to anyone but the emergency personnel.

A van made its way through the crowd, pulling to a stop in front of the hotel. Two men garbed in the heavily padded and armored bomb protection suits lumbered clumsily out of the van's side door. The last guy out reached back into the van and secured a toolbox. The two men entered the building.

So far, no explosions had gone off. Which meant the kid who'd entered wearing the bomb was still alive.

Danny hoped the bomb squad could get him out of the explosive vest and keep him alive. She turned and stood on her toes to look through the crowd of people. Still, she couldn't find Smoke or her uncle.

Several ambulances stood in a line in the parking lot in front of the hotel. Some victims of the crush were being treated or loaded into the backs of the vehicles.

Danny hurried toward them, asking the emergency personnel if they'd seen Ambassador Turner.

No one had seen the US Ambassador or her fiancé.

Another ambulance stood several yards from the others.

The back door was closed, but a light shone from within.

As Danny approached, a man came near her.

"Are you Ms. Turner, the US Ambassador's niece?" he asked.

Danny nodded. "I am. Have you seen him or my fiancé, the man who was with him?"

The man nodded. "Your uncle is inside the ambulance. They're trying to stabilize him. Do you want to stay with him?"

What she wanted was to find Smoke.

"Your fiancé left in an ambulance already," the man said. "If you want, you can ride with your uncle to the hospital."

Her heart pounded hard against her ribs. "What's wrong with my fiancé?"

"I wouldn't know," the man said. "I wasn't the one working on him. Are you coming with us or staying here? We need to get going."

Danny nodded. "I'll ride with my uncle."

The EMT opened the door.

A man inside leaned forward with his hand outstretched.

Danny automatically placed her hand in his. As he pulled her into the back of the ambulance, she caught sight of an empty stretcher. "Hey, where's my unc—"

The man behind her climbed up into the back with her, and the door slammed shut.

Danny went into survival mode and lashed out, hitting the man in front of her in the nose with the butt of her palm. He yelled, clutching his hands to his nose. She tried to kick him in the groin, but the cramped quarters didn't give her much room to work. Arms clamped around her, trapping hers to her sides. Then the man whose nose she'd busted flung a sheet over her head.

The ambulance lurched and rolled away from the hotel. She couldn't let them take her. She didn't know what was happening with Smoke and her uncle. They needed her.

When the man holding her arms to her sides released her for a second, she fought like a wild cat, only succeeding in getting more and more tangled in the sheet. The ambulance bumped and swayed, sending her flying into the one man, slamming into the sidewall and falling to her knees. The men cursed, then a ripping sound was followed by her arms once again being trapped at her sides. Then she was spun in a circle as what felt like thick tape was tightly wrapped around her body, pinning her arms to her sides and securing her legs together. She'd lost both her heels, and she couldn't see a thing with the sheet covering her face.

Danny was lifted and dropped onto the empty stretcher and strapped down. No amount of strength or self-defense training was going to get her out of this. Someone would have to cut her loose before she could help herself. Her first instinct was to fall back into victim mode and sink deep into a dark place where depression would suck the life out of her before anyone had a chance to kill her.

She couldn't go there. No. She *wouldn't* go there. When Danny had started down the path of rediscovering her inner strength, she'd decided she had too much to live for. She would escape. And when she did, she'd take some of these bastards down in the process.

CHAPTER 11

THE BOMB SQUAD came and took their sweet time disarming the wires from the vest and the grenade. All the while, Smoke forced himself to remain calm. It helped that his buddies talked to him the entire time via the communications device in his ear.

"We have the ambassador with us," Ketch had let him know as soon as they'd found the man wandering around the outside of the hotel, desperately searching for his niece.

"Danny?" Smoke asked.

Ketch's hesitation left a lead weight at the pit of Smoke's belly. "We haven't found her yet. The Prime Minister has his people calling all the nearby hospitals. They'll let us know as soon as they find her."

Being trapped with the kid and the explosives

made Smoke crazy with frustration. He needed to be out there, searching for Danny. But he couldn't. Not when the kid and the bomb squad technicians' lives hung in the balance. The number of explosives attached to the boy's vest was enough to level a city block. He used the quiet time to run through the scenarios of what could have happened to Danny. Nothing made sense. She wouldn't have left on her own. The only other explanation for her disappearance was that she'd been taken. But why? And by whom?

She wasn't one of the high-powered diplomats with a huge bank account that could be tapped for ransom. From what Smoke had observed, her family wasn't well enough off to have large amounts of cash that could be easily accessed. She hadn't been with the MMA long enough to amass a fortune doing sponsored ads. The only thing going for her was that she was an American. But then so was her uncle, and he was more politically significant than her.

When the bomb squad finally removed the grenade from the boy's and Smoke's hands, Smoke set the boy on his own feet, bent and stared into the child's tear-streaked face. "You're a brave man. You did good."

He turned and jogged out of the ballroom, down the stairs and out into the open, where he met up with his team and Ambassador Turner. His brothers clapped him on the back and pulled him into hug after hug until he held up his hands. "We can't celebrate until we have Danny back."

"We've been all around the exterior of the building. One of the EMTs said he spoke with a woman meeting Danny's description. He remembers her asking if he'd seen the American Ambassador. He saw her go from ambulance to ambulance." Ketch snored. "The guy said she wouldn't stop looking. She was so beautiful, which was to her benefit, because he said she climbed into the back of one of the ambulances, and it drove off."

"So, she could be at one of the hospitals," Smoke said.

"The Prime Minister promised to let us know as soon as he knows which one she was taken to," Ambassador Turner said. His cellphone chose that moment to ring. He glanced down at the caller ID. "It's the Prime Minister." He pressed the talk button, held the device to his ear and listened. "Thank you for going to the extra effort." Turner ended the call. "One of the ambulances was reported missing."

Smoke's hopes sank further.

"They found it abandoned in an empty church parking lot. No one saw anyone or anything."

"She had to be in that ambulance," Smoke said. "Were any other people reported missing from the guest list?"

"I asked the police who were managing the evacuation," Ketch said. "No one else has been reported missing."

"Why Danny?" the ambassador asked.

"I had the same question," Smoke said. "Could it be she was targeted for human trafficking?"

"If that were the case, what about the other beautiful women at the event?" Ice argued. "I saw quite a few coming out of the building."

"A crime of opportunity?" Ketch suggested.

Smoke paced a few yards away and back. "Has any group claimed responsibility for the attempted bombing?"

"I checked with my staff," Turner said. "Hamas was quick to say they were disappointed the entire hotel wasn't blown off the map with the Prime Minister and all his ministers with it. And they repeated their demand for their ship full of supplies and their threat for retribution against the Israelis and the US."

"They really want what's on that ship," Smoke noted.

The ambassador crossed his arms over his chest. "There's no way the Israelis are going to hand over a ship full of arms to Hamas in Gaza. They found arms buried beneath some of the boxes of medical supplies. They're going through each of the boxes now to make certain there aren't more arms hidden inside."

Smoke looked around. Most of the guests had dispersed. Once the building had been declared secure, they were allowed back in to collect their belongings and leave.

"I see no need to hang around here. I think she was on that ambulance."

"And we have no idea where she is now," her uncle said, his brow furrowed. "Where do we start?"

"I'll send some of our guys to the location where they found the ambulance and see if there are any security cameras in the area," Ketch said.

Smoke couldn't stand doing nothing. She'd disappeared completely. Other than the possibility of cameras being in the location where the ambulance was abandoned, they had no other clues to go on.

"Come back to the embassy with me," the ambassador said.

Smoke knew he had to. Danny would want him to make sure her uncle was safe before he started looking for her. "Okay. We'll get you back, and then I'm going to turn this city upside down until I find her."

THOUGH SHE COULDN'T SEE where they were going, Danny focused on anything that would help her know where they were taking her. She hadn't recognized the men who'd captured her. They had worn matching polo shirts like the ones worn by the other ambulance drivers. She'd had no reason to suspect they weren't what she thought they were. Even so, she kicked herself for letting them lure her into the ambulance and secure her so effectively she couldn't begin to work her way free.

They'd stopped long enough to transfer her from the ambulance into the trunk of a car. When they closed the lid, what little light had filtered through the white sheet was gone, and now, she lay in the dark, listening and thinking about the path they were taking. So far, they'd driven slowly, making a lot of turns, as if weaving through older, narrower streets or residential neighborhoods. They stopped briefly. The muffled sound of metal cranking slowly made her think of a gate opening. When the car pulled forward, the metal cranking sound repeated—definitely a gate.

The car stopped.

Danny heard the hum of a garage door opening. When it stopped, the car moved forward, stopped, and then the engine shut off. The garage door closed, and the car doors opened and closed.

Footsteps rounded to the back of the vehicle, and the trunk lid opened.

Meaty arms lifted her out of the trunk. She was flung over a man's shoulder and carried through a door, down a flight of stairs and into a musty, darker place. A basement?

She was dumped onto a cold hard floor, her body hitting hard, her head bouncing against concrete. Something sharp poked into her side and tore through the tape holding her arms against her sides. As soon as her arms were free, she bent her bound legs and kicked them at the man hovering over her. Her feet hit something hard. A crashing sound was followed by muttered curses.

Danny fought the sheet, ripping it over her head and flinging it to the side. With her legs still bound together with duct tape, she couldn't get up and run.

The big man who'd brought her there scrambled to his feet.

Danny cocked her legs again, waited for him to get close enough, and then kicked out.

He dodged her blow, caught her feet, yanked hard and slid her across the floor toward him.

She punched, scratched and tried to poke him in the eyes. Without her legs to work with, she was limited on what she could do, and running wasn't an option.

She landed a solid kick with both feet to the man's groin.

He growled and backhanded her with all the force of a man big enough to throw telephone poles.

The blow caught Danny across her cheekbone and made her head snap back and hit the concrete floor. Stars glittered around the edges of her vision, and the room spun.

Unable to focus or think, she wasn't ready when he clamped his arms around her, lifted her and sat her in a chair. Another man entered the room. While the first guy held her in place, the other one wrapped a strand of duct tape around her arms and the back of the chair.

She sat still, gathering her scrambled senses. Her head ached, and warm liquid dripped down the side of her cheek where the bruiser had clocked her. If she ever got completely loose, she'd show him she wasn't afraid.

He lifted her, chair and all, and carried her to a bare patch of floor beneath a lamp hanging from the ceiling. Then they climbed the stairs out of the basement, leaving her alone.

Danny struggled against the duct tape, bending her wrist to reach up with her fingers to tug at it, tearing it with her fingernails. She got a small strand of the thick tape loose, and was working on more, when the door at the top of the stairs opened. Footsteps sounded on the stairs, and legs encased in black trousers came into view. A smaller man than the one who'd carried her down there came into view, wearing a black scarf around his face and a black turban. He stopped in front of her and stared down at her with eyes so dark they appeared black. In his hand, he held a sheet of paper. He shoved it toward her and said, "You will make this statement in front of the world," he said in a deep voice that didn't sound at all natural.

She stared at the page, reading the words, her stomach roiling as she understood the message's meaning. "You want me to say my government is corrupt and is stealing medical supplies from the children of Gaza. And if they don't allow the ship carrying the supplies to complete its mission, you will behead me in front of the people of the world. Me losing my head will be in trade for the lives of the children my country has condemned to their deaths. Do I understand that correctly?"

"Yes."

"How long will you give them to comply?" she asked.

"Two hours," he responded. The man was purposely disguising his voice by making it deeper.

Danny had the distinct feeling that she knew this man. She needed to hear him speak in his natural voice. She shook her head. "Two hours wouldn't get the ship out of the harbor, much less all the way over to Gaza."

"Two hours to respond, six hours to deliver."

"And at what point will you free me?" she demanded.

"When the ship and its entire cargo are safely in

the port of Gaza." He wasn't dropping the fake voice.

Danny would have to get him excited or angry to make him throw caution to the wind and use his natural voice. She stared up at the man, meeting his gaze unflinchingly. "No."

He carefully laid the page on a table behind him and turned back to her. "You would risk losing your pretty head over a single message?"

"You'd risk angering my country by beheading one of its citizens? You must either be very brave or very stupid." She sneered. "I'm going to go with stupid."

The man's eyes flared, and he struck out, slapping her so hard across her cheek, her head whipped around. "You will deliver this message if I have to knock every one of your teeth from your head." He'd dropped the deep fake voice and was speaking closer to what Danny would think was normal. She knew that voice but was having a hard time identifying it, as if she hadn't heard it often but, perhaps, recently.

She needed to keep him talking until she had it. "You realize my country doesn't bargain with terrorists."

He snorted. "Then we're wasting our time, and you're of no use to me."

"If you behead me, I will become a martyr, and your cause will be lost. The world will see Hamas as barbaric terrorists and hunt them into extinction. And we're back to the fact that you're stupid."

This time he punched her in the jaw, making her teeth rattle. She'd had worse in the MMA ring. This guy wasn't used to doing his own dirty work. He paid others to do it for him. Which meant he had money.

Her breath caught and held. She stared at the dark eyes revealed through the slit in the scarf. Above those dark eyes were heavy dark brows. He wasn't terribly tall, and if she was free to move about, she could knock him on his ass. Like she had before.

It came to her in a flash, along with how she could possibly save herself and get this man captured and sent to jail for the terrorist he was. But she couldn't cave to his demands too easily, which meant she had to take a few more beatings for the team.

So be it.

CHAPTER 12

SMOKE PACED the length of Ambassador Turner's office for the fifteenth time. It had been two hours since Danny had disappeared from the hotel.

"We combed the area where the ambulance had been found and didn't find a single security camera," Ketch said.

"Not one," Gonzo agreed. "They chose the switch site for that reason. No cameras and no witnesses."

"We have nothing," Smoke said. And he'd failed her completely. What kind of protection detail lost the one he was supposed to protect?

"The Prime Minister is having the ambulance dusted for fingerprints. He'll notify us if or when they find a match," the ambassador said.

He started across the floor again, unable to stand still; he needed action. "There has to be more that we can do. If we only had a hint of a clue. Something, anything."

"Holy shit." Ice looked up from his cellphone. "Look at this. No, wait, turn on the news. Hurry."

The ambassador grabbed a remote control from his desktop and hit the ON button. The television mounted on the wall blinked to life on a local news channel.

What Smoke saw nearly brought him to his knees.

"Danny," he said.

"This is Danica Turner." She stared at the camera, her face bruised, a cut on her cheek and her sandy-blond hair in disarray. She paused, blinked several times then dragged in a deep breath.

God, she looked like hell, and yet she was the most beautiful woman Smoke could imagine. His heart squeezed hard in his chest.

Speaking slowly, she continued, "My government is holding hostage important medical supplies for the children of Gaza."

Again, she paused and blinked into the camera before returning her attention to whatever she was reading from on the table in front of her.

"If they do not allow the ship containing the supplies to complete its mission, the leaders of Hamas will behead me in front of the people of the world in exchange for the lives of the many children my country has condemned to their deaths." She looked into the camera as if she were staring right into Smoke's eyes and blinked.

"You have two hours to make your decision known. Or my head rolls. Then you will have six hours to deliver on your promise." She blinked again, but the video feed was cut off.

"Oh, my dear sweet niece." Ambassador Turner scrubbed a hand down his face. "They must've hit her hard. Did you see how many times she blinked?" He shook his head.

"Can you play the feed again," Smoke said. He stepped closer to the screen and studied everything about the video, from the background to the sounds, and then Danny's face. Something bothered him. Mostly, her expression was set in a grim mask, almost stoic. Except for the blinking. Yes, they'd been rough with her, but she was a former MMA fighter. Getting hit was part of the game. And the blinking... What would cause her to blink? And it was only when she paused to take a breath that she blinked more. Could it be...

"Play it again," he said, his voice terse. He grabbed a pen and notepad from the ambassador's desktop. This time when Danny blinked, he copied the pattern in dashes and dots.

Gonzo leaned over Smoke's shoulder. "Son of a bitch. She didn't."

"Didn't what?" the ambassador said.

The men all gathered around Smoke as he completed the pattern. "Ice, pull up the Morse code chart. I know it, but not well enough to do this quickly."

Ice brought up the chart, and they quickly decoded Danny's blinks.

Smoke glanced up at the ambassador. "We need the local address for Benjamin Cohen—ASAP. You heard your niece. We have less than two hours to find Cohen and get Danny out. In the meantime, contact the US State Department and start negotiations to get those medical supplies to the Port of Gaza in case we don't get there in time." Smoke glanced around at his team. "Who's with me?"

"Seriously?" Voodoo shook his head. "You have to ask?"

"This will be an unsanctioned mission. If we get caught, Cohen has clout in a lot of places. He could turn the tables on us and paint us as having gone rogue. Even our command wouldn't be able to bail us out."

Ketch nodded. "All the more reason to do it right."

"It's what we do best," Gonzo said. "Get in, get the girl and get out. No problem."

"Ready to go in fifteen?" Smoke asked.

"Meet in the parking lot of the hotel across from the embassy," Ketch said.

Ketch, Voodoo, Ice, Gonzo and Rome hurried out of the ambassador's office.

Smoke faced Danny's uncle. "Are you okay with our plan?"

He gave a hint of a smile. "I'm sure we're going against all protocol, but I don't give a damn. We need to do whatever it takes to get Danny back alive."

"If this goes sideways, I'll swear on a stack of Bibles you knew nothing about our plan."

"Son, I don't expect that. If it goes sideways, I'll take my share of the blame. Besides, it might be time for me to retire anyway. I'll text the address to you." He gave Smoke a chin lift. "Go. Get our Danny."

Smoke spun and ran from the room, taking the stairs up to his apartment where he changed into dark cargo pants, a dark shirt and grabbed his equipment bag containing his rifle, body armor, helmet and ammunition. He was back down the stairs in less than five minutes and left the embassy compound.

His team was already gathered around the van they'd rented. The hatch was up, and all their equipment bags were piled inside.

Ketch took the driver's seat, Smoke claimed shotgun and the rest piled into the back.

Smoke pulled out his cellphone. Ambassador Turner had texted the address to him. He entered it into the map application, and they set off to rescue the woman who'd captured Smoke's heart and soul.

A hard knot formed in Smoke's chest. The price of failure was the death of a courageous woman who'd managed to send the information they needed to save her. For Smoke, failure was not an option.

No pressure.

LEFT on her own in the basement, Danny worked at the tape trapping her in the chair she'd been placed in over an hour ago. She'd torn halfway through the tape behind her and struggled to reach the rest. It was taking too much time. She needed to be free sooner. If her Morse code message hadn't been detected, she had to get herself out of Cohen's basement on her own.

Frustrated at the slow progress, she tried standing. Because the chair had a back, when she stood, she was bent over. It took several attempts before she was up and steady. Now what? She couldn't just walk around. Her legs were still bound with tape.

Maybe, if she broke the chair, she could free her arms and hands. Danny hopped in a circle, scoping out the basement. Once she'd located the nearest wall, she hopped toward it. Several times, she almost lost her balance but quickly regained it. When she reached the wall, she tried slamming the chair's legs sideways against the stone. The legs remained intact. Hopping around so that her back was to the wall, she threw herself backward, bounced off the wall and fell sideways. The legs on one side broke off.

Rising to her feet again, she flung herself backward at an angle. The other legs broke off the chair. Still stuck with the seat and back, she sat flat on the floor and pushed backward. The wood creaked and cracked.

Danny tried again. This time, the back broke away from the seat. Danny grabbed the chair back with her fingertips and pulled, twisting her upper body at the same time. On the edge of giving up, the chair back fell free of the tape, loosening its hold on Danny's upper arms. Moments later, she wiggled her arms and body out of the remaining loop and reached for the tape wrapped around her legs.

Danny leaped to her feet and made a quick pass through the basement, looking for a window or secret passage but finding nothing. The staircase and door at the top were her only way out.

Easing to the top of the stairs, she pressed her ear to the wooden panel and listened. When she didn't hear anything, she wrapped her hand around the doorknob and twisted. As she'd suspected, it was locked. She hurried back down the steps and searched through an array of tools and junk until she found a crowbar. Back up the stairs, she fit the crowbar into the narrow gap between the door and the frame, just below the doorknob and pushed slowly, adding pressure until the door frame split. She stopped and listened again for any sounds on the other side.

Again, she applied the crowbar. This time, the door separated from the frame and swung toward her.

She backed up and let it open all the way. With the crowbar in her hand, she emerged into a shiny, gourmet kitchen fit for a billionaire. She bet he didn't prepare any of his meals. And if that was the case, he'd given his staff, less his thugs, the night off.

Speaking of thugs, they couldn't be far, not with a captive in the basement they'd have to check on when the mandated two hours were up. The time had come to close. She was almost certain the US government wouldn't respond to demands that quickly. She hoped that her Deltas would. She could use a little help extricating herself from the billionaire's clutches. Although she was doing well on her own, she couldn't bank on making it out of his mansion undetected. As wealthy as he was, or had been, the place had to be set up with security cameras. Someone somewhere would be watching and would alert the boss as soon as they saw her sneaking about.

Being barefoot was an advantage in the house. When she made it outside, she might not feel the same. She'd cross that bridge barefooted when the time came.

Danny eased open the swinging door from the kitchen into the dining room. She opened it just enough to peek through.

The two men who'd brought her there sat at the polished mahogany table, drinking coffee and staring at their cellphones.

Danny backed away from the door and turned toward the back door leading out of the kitchen. She hurried across the floor, twisted the deadbolt and pulled open the door.

An alarm screamed.

Someone shouted from the dining room, and Danny dove through the door and into a four-car garage. She slammed the door shut behind her and frantically searched the wall for the button to open one of the overhead doors.

When she did find one, she punched it and ran toward the moving door. Of course, it was the one on the far end of the garage, and three cars stood between her and her escape. She ran, dodged and prayed she'd make it out before the men caught up to her.

Halfway across the massive garage, the far door stopped going up and started going down.

No!

Danny ran faster. She reached the door with only a couple of feet of clearance remaining. She threw herself onto the ground and rolled beneath the door. The motion sensor triggered, and the door began to rise.

Danny leaped to her feet and ran around the side of the house to avoid being shot. It was then that she realized a six-foot stucco wall surrounded the house. She ran toward it and tried to leap up onto it. It was too high. She placed her hand on top of the wall and tried to pull herself up. The wall was rounded on the edge and provided nothing for her to grip to leverage her body up to the top. Footsteps sounded around the side of the garage.

Danny ran along the wall, hoping to find something she could climb to get her to the top. Ahead on a stone patio, she spotted several potted plants. After pushing one of the pots over, she rolled it to the wall. Then she stepped up onto the pot and swung her leg up. About to hoist her body onto the wall, she was yanked down by a hand on her ankle.

She landed hard on the ground and looked up into Benjamin Cohen's face.

He stood over her, pointing a pistol at her chest. "You are proving to be more trouble than you're worth."

"Why?" she asked. "Why are you interested in that ship making it to Gaza?"

"I paid for those supplies," he said. "And I don't get paid until they reach the customer."

She frowned up at him. "You're a rich man. What's one shipment?"

"You know nothing about the world," he said. "I've spent the last twenty years forming alliances, building an empire. Suddenly, those alliances dissolve, and the money, time and effort I've poured into them are gone. And with them, the money I earned through my hard work."

"And the work of children mining your diamonds. Not to mention the corruption you propagated with the former leader of the DRC."

"It's business."

"Until the world's leaders catch on and freeze your bank accounts." She sat up. "Is that it? You had it all, and you lost it all. So, you turned to the lucrative business of illegal arms trade to terrorists?"

"They're only terrorists if you're on the other side," he said. "It doesn't matter. Your two hours are up. Your country doesn't give a damn about what happens to you. I'll serve you up on the Hamas plate with one of their favorite demonstrations of dominance. Horam! Jazeel!"

Danny glanced in the direction of the garage, expecting the two big men to already be on their way to do their boss's bidding.

They weren't there.

When Cohen glanced around to locate his men,

Danny made her move. She swept her leg out, catching Cohen's ankles.

He tipped over, firing off a shot as he fell.

Danny leaped to her feet, ready to run.

Three men in black flew over the wall and landed on the ground, surrounding Danny. They wore battle gear and helmets. She didn't know if they were friends or foes until one of them spoke.

"Danny," Smoke said.

Cohen rolled onto his back and pointed his gun at Danny.

Without hesitating, Smoke kicked the man's wrist, sending the gun flying through the air. It landed on the flagstone patio, well out of the man's reach.

From around the corner of the garage, three more Deltas arrived, leading the two men who'd captured Danny and brought her to Cohen's compound.

"Our Israeli Special Forces counterparts are on their way to claim this victory," Ketch said. "They were a bit pissed we didn't include them in the fun."

"I'm sure they'll get over it when they realize we've nailed a traitor in their midst," Smoke said.

Gonzo lifted Cohen to his feet and secured his hands behind his back with a zip-tie.

Smoke pulled Danny into his arms and kissed her hard. "You're a genius."

She smiled up at him. "You got my message."

He nodded. "We're here, aren't we?"

"Yes, you are." Danny grinned, happily. "So, who figured it out first?" she asked.

The team, as one, said, "Smoke!"

"Did you learn Morse code in the Army?" Ketch asked.

Danny shook her head. "Not actually. My father taught me all the good things. Morse code was just one of them."

"I like your father already," Smoke said.

Danny beamed. "I think my father would like you, too." She looked around at the Deltas. "Thank you all."

"No man left behind," Smoke said. "Or woman. You're one of us, now.

EPILOGUE

"THANKS FOR COMING HOME WITH ME," Danny said as she stood in Smoke's arms on the back porch of her father's house. "These past two weeks have been heaven."

"I'm glad you invited me. And I think your uncle is glad he came, too."

She chuckled. "It's like Uncle James is ten years younger since coming here."

"I think he'll like retirement in Michigan," Smoke said.

"Think they'll miss us when we leave?" she asked, wrapping her arms around his waist.

"Absolutely." Smoke's lips twisted. "Who else will they have to laugh at when I fall out of the kayak?"

"You were pretty hilarious," she said. "I still think you did it on purpose."

"I wish I could lie and say that was my plan." He sighed. "Alas, I need a little more practice in the kayak before you turn me loose on the lake."

"Deal." She wrapped her hand around the back of his neck and pulled him down to kiss her.

Smoke crushed her to him, deepening the kiss, sweeping her tongue in a long, sensual caress.

He loved being with this woman and loved her family, and he wanted to make it permanent. He'd waited until the last day of their vacation to do what he had to do. He couldn't wait any longer. It was time.

He broke off the kiss, leaned back and looked into her eyes. "Danny, I've got something I need to tell you."

Her brow puckered. "That's funny. I have something I need to tell you."

"You first," they said as one.

Smoke chuckled. "I'll go first before I lose my nerve." He fished in his pocket for the ring, nearly having a panic attack when he didn't find it. Then he switched to the other pocket, found the ring and sighed. "Danny…" He paused. "No, this isn't right."

"You're killing me, Asher."

"I have to do this right." He dropped to one knee and looked up at her. "Danica Turner—"

"Danny! Where'd you put my fishing pole?" Daniel Turner came around the corner of the house, carrying a tackle box and wearing his favorite fishing hat. He took one look and said, "Oops. Sorry. Don't mind me." He performed an about-face and started back the opposite direction.

"Hey, Dan, are we going fishing or not? We only have a couple more hours of daylight." James Turner rounded the corner of the house, wearing cargo pants, a Detroit Lions sweatshirt and a fishing hat just like his brother's.

Daniel hooked his brother's arm and tried to spin him around. "Shhh. He's about to pop the question. Let's give them some privacy."

Smoke looked up at Danny. "Do you mind?"

She shook her head. "Not at all. I think they should be here."

Smoke nodded. "Hey, you two, stick around for the show."

The older men spun and came back to stand on the ground below the deck.

"About time you got around to it," Daniel muttered. "He asked me a week ago."

"He asked me back in Israel," James said

Daniel glared at his brother. "Whose kid is she?"

"I love you both," Danny said. "Now, let the man have his say. I'm not getting any younger."

Smoke laughed at how quickly the old guys shut their yaps. "As I was saying... Danica Turner, I didn't think I needed anyone in my life until you came along and showed me just how much I was missing. I love that you're strong, independent, kickass and most of all…loving. It would make me the happiest man alive if you would agree to marry me."

She smiled down at him and brought him to his feet. "I love you, Asher Gray. I can't imagine my life without you in it. Yes. I'm honored that you picked me, and I promise to love you forever and more."

Smoke slipped the ring on her finger, and then they kissed. His heart was so full he could barely breathe. He laughed. "I almost forgot…you had something you wanted to tell me?"

She nodded and looked up into his eyes, hers shining with moisture. "Can we make the wedding soon? Like really soon?"

He smiled. "Of course. I'll take you to the justice of the peace tomorrow if it made you happy. Why?"

"I don't know when or how it happened, but I'm pregnant. You're going to be a daddy."

Joy spread like wildfire through Smoke's heart. "A daddy? Me? You?" He wrapped his arms around her and swung her through the air. When he set her back on her feet, he turned to their audience. "Did you hear that? I'm going to be a daddy!"

"Congratulations," Daniel said.

James grinned. "I'm so happy for you both."

Daniel leaned toward his brother. "She told me yesterday."

"I knew the day before when I found the test stick," James said. "We're going to be grandfathers."

193

He pounded his brother on his back. "Now, let's go fishing."

Smoke led Danny over to the porch swing and sat beside her, staring out at the late afternoon sun shining across the water. "I never thought this would be me."

Danny laughed. "What? Sitting on a porch swing like a couple of old people?"

"That and sitting beside someone I love. I never thought I'd have that until I met you."

She leaned her head on his shoulder. "I know what you mean. Growing up, I thought I'd have that someday. Then life in the Army happened and I didn't think it was possible. I didn't think I was worthy." Danny squeezed his arm. "Then you came along, and I realized I could have that kind of love."

"Sweetheart, you're worthy. Don't let anyone make you think otherwise. And you deserve to be happy and loved." He turned and kissed her forehead. "And you're going to make one helluva a mother. Our baby is going to be the luckiest kid ever."

SAVING KYLA

BROTHERHOOD PROTECTORS
COLORADO BOOK #1

New York Times & *USA Today*
Bestselling Author

ELLE JAMES

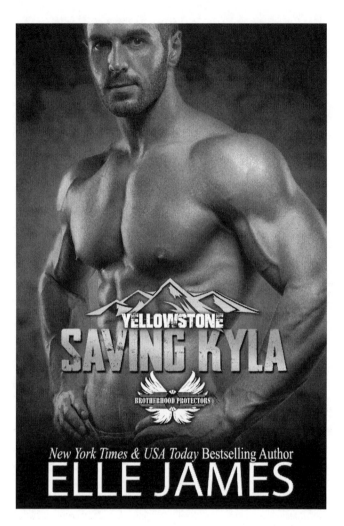

YELLOWSTONE
SAVING KYLA
BROTHERHOOD PROTECTORS

New York Times & USA Today Bestselling Author
ELLE JAMES

CHAPTER 1

KYLA RUSSELL WAS DONE with killing.

Especially when her target didn't deserve to die.

Camouflaged as an Afghan male in a long white thobe, the ankle-length white shirt Afghan men wore, she stood on a street in Kandahar, Afghanistan, a pistol with a silencer attached strapped to her thigh. Beneath the thobe, she wore dark jeans and a dark shirt for night movement.

She'd pulled her long, black hair up and wrapped it in a dark turban like the ones worn by men in the city. To complete her disguise, she'd applied a fake beard, bushy eyebrows and dark makeup to make her appear more masculine and able to walk freely around the city of over six hundred thousand people.

Kyla had spent the better part of the day before studying her target, both through the windows of his home and by tailing him as he'd left for work and returned. What about this man made him toxic? Why had her government deemed him dangerous to the world?

She made it a priority to research her assignments, to find out about the persons she was assigned to eliminate. Prior to accepting her current mission, she'd reviewed the dossier her handler had given her for Abdul Naser Ahmadi and had done her own background check on the man via her connections on the internet and the Dark Web.

The dossier had listed Ahmadi as an arms trafficker, supplying American weapons to the Taliban. Nothing in Kyla's own research indicated the same. In fact, Ahmadi was like a black hole of information. All she could find was that he lived with his wife in Kandahar and worked at a local university as a professor of language and literature.

Kyla had no qualms about ridding the world of pedophiles or people who tortured and killed others for their race or religious beliefs. She'd taken out cult leaders who'd planned terrorist activities in the United States and some who were killers in foreign countries.

Some of her targets had been dirty politicians, selling secrets to US enemies, placing her country's military in jeopardy. Those targets, she'd taken out with no problem and no regrets. The world was a better place without them.

Kyla took pride in never completing a mission without first understanding the target and the necessity of taking him out.

Ahmadi was not raising any red flags. Still, she planned to observe the man for a couple of days in case she was wrong.

Standing on a street corner, her back to the wall of a building, she casually observed Ahmadi at a local tea shop where he sat with another man. Maybe this was the reason for the hit—this meeting with Ahmadi's guest.

Using her cellphone, Kyla snapped a picture of the man and sent it to her contact on the Dark Web, who had access to facial recognition software.

Within minutes she was surprised to receive a response.

Jalal Malik CIA.

Kyla frowned at the message. *CIA? What the hell?*

Kyla sent the picture of Malik and Ahmadi along with a message to an old friend she'd known from her days in the CIA. A man who had access to more than he should.

Jalal Malik CIA...Legit? Clean?

Her contact responded several minutes later:

Born in the US to first-generation Afghans who escaped Afghanistan and Taliban rule thirty years before and earned their US citizenship. Malik speaks fluent Pashto and joined the CIA to give back to the country that saved his parents. Now working to uncover a mole in the US government, who is feeding information and arms to the Taliban. Ahmadi is his trusted informant.

With Ahmadi in her sights, Kyla could have picked him off any time that day and disappeared. However, she couldn't pull the trigger, not when her gut told her something was off. Ahmadi wasn't dangerous to the US. In fact, his willingness to help the US find the traitor within made him an asset and put him in danger of Taliban retaliation. Why had he been targeted for extermination?

She'd followed him home to ask him that question. By the time he'd returned to his home, darkness had settled over Kandahar.

Kyla ducked into the shadows of the wall surrounding Ahmadi's home, where she stripped out of the white thobe and trousers and tucked them behind a stack of stones. Then she pulled herself up and over the wall, dropped down into Ahmadi's yard and watched for her chance to corner the target.

That chance presented itself within the hour.

Ahmadi's wife had gone to the bedroom. Ahmadi stepped out his back door onto the hard-packed dirt within the stone wall to smoke a cigarette.

Kyla slipped up behind him, clamped her hand

over his mouth and pressed a pistol with the silencer attachment to his temple. She lowered her voice and spoke in Pashto, "Tell me why my government wants you dead."

He stood still, making no attempt to fight back. "Who is your government?"

She nudged his temple with the pistol. "The same government who sent your guest at tea."

He nodded and switched to English. "Perhaps we are getting too close to the truth," he said in a whisper.

Kyla released the man and stepped back, her weapon trained on Ahmadi's chest as he turned to face her, his hands raised.

"I am not your enemy," he said.

"Then why would my government send me to kill you?" she asked.

He shook his head. "For the same reason I had tea with another citizen of your country. One of your own is playing for the other side and has sent you to do his dirty work."

"What do you know that would make someone put a hit out on you?" she asked.

"If you will not kill me, I will tell you what I told my guest at tea." Ahmadi's eyes narrowed as he awaited her response.

Kyla lowered her weapon. She could still kill him if he made a move to hurt her.

Ahmadi drew in a deep breath and let it out

slowly before speaking again. "I received the name of the man who has been coordinating shipments to the Taliban. He goes by…Abaddon."

"Abaddon?"

The man nodded. "The meaning of the name is destruction."

At that moment, Ahmadi's wife called out in Pashto, "Are you expecting a delivery? A van just arrived in front of our gate."

Ahmadi glanced toward the house.

A knot of foreboding formed in Kyla's gut. "Call your wife to you."

Ahmadi frowned. "Why?"

"Just do it. Now." Kyla turned and slipped between the wall and the house.

Behind her, Ahmadi called to his wife.

Through the windows, Kyla could see Ahmadi's wife moving toward the back of the house.

Kyla slowed at the front corner and peered through the wrought iron gate at a dark van parked on the street. A door opened, and a man dressed in dark clothes and a ski mask dropped down.

If the mask wasn't enough to make her blood run cold, the mini machine gun he carried did the trick.

Kyla's pulse slammed through her veins. She spun and raced to the back of the house, where Ahmadi and his wife stood together.

Kyla glanced at the wall she'd scaled easily.

Ahmadi and his wife would not go over it as quickly, dressed as they were in long robes.

In Pashto, she said, "Over the wall. Hurry." She bent and cupped her hands.

Ahmadi urged his wife to go first.

She hung back.

"Go," Kyla urged. "Or we all die."

The woman stepped into Kyla's palms. With her husband pushing from behind, she landed on her stomach and swung her leg over the top of the stone wall. She dropped to the other side.

Kyla held her hands for Ahmadi.

"No, you go first," Ahmadi said.

"No time to argue," she remained bent over.

Ahmadi stepped into her hands.

Kyla straightened.

Ahmadi pulled himself up to the top of the wall and reached down to give her a hand up.

She shook her head. "Go!"

He slipped over the wall and dropped to the ground on the other side.

Doors slammed open inside the house as the man in the black ski mask worked his way through the rooms. It wouldn't take him long. The house wasn't that big.

Kyla got a short, running start, scaled the wall and slung her leg over.

As she slipped over the top, she glanced back. The man in the black ski mask had just reached the back door and flung it open. Before he could see her, she dropped to the other side.

Her turban caught on a crack in the wall. Unable to stop and free it, she let it go, the ponytail she'd wound around her head shaking loose. She didn't have time to retrieve her thobe. It didn't matter. Without the turban, the disguise was useless. All she could do was run. She raced after Ahmadi and his wife.

They ran for several city blocks. The couple wouldn't be able to keep up the pace for long.

Kyla glanced over her shoulder. The man in black rounded a corner and sprinted toward them.

"Turn left," Kyla yelled to the couple. They did, and Kyla followed. "Keep going and find a safe place to hide. I'll take care of him." She stopped running and waited for the assassin to catch up.

Ahmadi and his wife turned another corner, zigzagging through the streets.

Kyla waited, her gun poised and ready. When the man didn't burst around the corner as she expected, she eased her head around.

Several yards away, the man was climbing into the van's passenger side. Once he was in, the van leaped forward, headed for her corner.

Kyla aimed at the driver's windshield and fired.

Her bullet pierced the window.

The van swerved and then straightened, coming straight for her position on the corner.

She fired again.

This time the van swerved and slid sideways into a building.

The man in the ski mask jumped out of the passenger side and, using the door for cover, aimed his rifle at Kyla.

Knowing her pistol didn't have the range or accuracy of the shooter's rifle, she backed away from the corner and ran. She had to get to a better position to defend herself or get the hell away.

She was halfway to the next corner when tires squealed behind her.

A glance over her shoulder confirmed...the van was back in action and barreling toward her.

In front of her, headlights flashed as a small sedan turned onto the street. A man leaned out of the passenger window with a rifle and fired at her.

Fuck.

The bullets hit the pavement beside her. Kyla turned right onto the street nearest her and ducked behind the first home she came to. She circled the house, leaping over piles of stones and brick, and hid in the shadows near the rear of the home as the sedan turned onto the street. The van was slowing as it approached the corner.

As the van turned, Kyla aimed at the front tire of the van and popped off a round. The tire blew and sent the van veering toward the front of the house behind which she hid and crashed into the front entrance.

Kyla didn't wait for the driver to recover. She backtracked and ran back in the direction from which she'd come, zigzagging between houses, hugging the shadows as she went. Several times, she was certain she glimpsed the sedan.

She hoped Ahmadi and his wife had made good their escape. After she'd split from them, she was certain the attackers had been after her. They had to know she wasn't Ahmadi. Her long ponytail would have given her away.

Making her way through the darkened streets, she pulled off the fake beard and eyebrows, wincing as the glue proved stubborn. She couldn't stay in Kandahar. Not dressed as she was. The Taliban patrolled the streets day and night, looking for people breaking the newly enforced laws. She would be arrested or beaten for her lack of appropriate attire.

Not knowing exactly who the attackers were, she couldn't afford to be caught. If they were members of the elite team of assassins she was a part of, they would know they were chasing her—and they were aiming for her, specifically.

As of that moment, she no longer worked for the US government. She was now a threat to the people who'd trained and recruited her. They'd be looking for her in Kandahar. She no longer had the support to get her out of the country. If she wanted out, she'd have to find her own way.

Double fuck.

Kyla made her way to the edge of the city, moving quickly. She had to get out before sunrise. She couldn't trust anyone. People wouldn't be willing to help her. Not a lone female without male protection. Especially dressed as a Westerner in pants, not wearing the mandated black abaya.

As she arrived on the edge of the city, she paused in the shadows of a fuel station.

A truck pulled up, loaded with bags of onions, oranges and various other produce. From the direction it had come, it was heading out of town for an early morning delivery.

Kyla waited for the driver to fill his tank and pay the attendant.

When he finally climbed back into the cab and started his engine, Kyla made her move.

The truck pulled out from beneath the light from a single bulb hanging over the pump and slowly picked up speed on the road heading west.

Kyla glanced left and then right.

The attendant had returned to the inside of the station. No other vehicles were in sight.

She took off, sprinting after the truck, grabbed the side rail and vaulted up into the back, landing on a stack of bagged oranges. Adjusting several heavy bags, she created a hole and fit herself into the middle, out of sight of other traffic that might pass them on the road. She settled back, praying when they stopped that she could find a way out of Afghanistan and back to the States.

Once there, she'd use her nefarious contacts in the Dark Web and her former colleagues in the CIA to find out what the hell had just happened.

THE BUMPY ROAD and the sway of the old vehicle must have lulled her to sleep.

When the truck slowed and made a couple of sharp turns, Kyla's eyes blinked, and she stared up at the sun beating down on her and the buildings on either side of the truck as it maneuvered into a small village at the edge of the hills. She guessed it was making a delivery stop, which meant she needed to get out before the driver brought the truck to a complete stop.

Kyla pushed the bags of oranges out of the way and scooted toward the tailgate. As the truck turned another corner, she dropped out of the back and rolled in the dust into the shadows, coming to a stop when she bumped up against a pair of boots.

ABOUT THE AUTHOR

ELLE JAMES also writing as MYLA JACKSON is a *New York Times* and *USA Today* Bestselling author of books including cowboys, intrigues and paranormal adventures that keep her readers on the edges of their seats. When she's not at her computer, she's traveling, snow skiing, boating, or riding her ATV, dreaming up new stories. Learn more about Elle James at www.ellejames.com

Website | Facebook | Twitter | GoodReads | Newsletter | BookBub | Amazon

Or visit her alter ego Myla Jackson at mylajackson.com
Website | Facebook | Twitter | Newsletter

Follow Me!
www.ellejames.com
ellejamesauthor@gmail.com

ALSO BY ELLE JAMES

Brotherhood Protectors International

Athens Affair (#1)

Belgian Betrayal (#2)

Croatia Collateral (#3)

Dublin Debacle (#4)

Edinburgh Escape (#5)

Brotherhood Protectors Hawaii

Kalea's Hero (#1)

Leilani's Hero (#2)

Kiana's Hero (#3)

Maliea's Hero (#4)

Emi's Hero (#5)

Sachie's Hero (#6)

Kimo's Hero (#7)

Alana's Hero (#8)

Nala's Hero (#9)

Mika's Hero (#10)

Bayou Brotherhood Protectors

Remy (#1)

Gerard (#2)

Lucas (#3)

Beau (#4)

Rafael (#5)

Valentin (#6)

Landry (#7)

Simon (#8)

Maurice (#9)

Jacques (#10)

Brotherhood Protectors Yellowstone

Saving Kyla (#1)

Saving Chelsea (#2)

Saving Amanda (#3)

Saving Liliana (#4)

Saving Breely (#5)

Saving Savvie (#6)

Saving Jenna (#7)

Saving Peyton (#8)

Saving Londyn (#9)

Brotherhood Protectors Colorado

SEAL Salvation (#1)

Rocky Mountain Rescue (#2)

Ranger Redemption (#3)

Breaking Silence (#1)

Breaking Rules (#2)

Breaking Away (#3)

Breaking Free (#4)

Breaking Hearts (#5)

Breaking Ties (#6)

Breaking Point (#7)

Breaking Dawn (#8)

Breaking Promises (#9)

Hearts & Heroes Series

Wyatt's War (#1)

Mack's Witness (#2)

Ronin's Return (#3)

Sam's Surrender (#4)

Hellfire Series

Hellfire, Texas (#1)

Justice Burning (#2)

Smoldering Desire (#3)

Hellfire in High Heels (#4)

Playing With Fire (#5)

Up in Flames (#6)

Total Meltdown (#7)

Take No Prisoners Series

SEAL's Honor (#1)

SEAL'S Desire (#2)

SEAL's Embrace (#3)

SEAL's Obsession (#4)

SEAL's Proposal (#5)

SEAL's Seduction (#6)

SEAL'S Defiance (#7)

SEAL's Deception (#8)

SEAL's Deliverance (#9)

SEAL's Ultimate Challenge (#10)

Texas Billionaire Club

Tarzan & Janine (#1)

Something To Talk About (#2)

Who's Your Daddy (#3)

Love & War (#4)

Billionaire Online Dating Service

The Billionaire Husband Test (#1)

The Billionaire Cinderella Test (#2)

The Billionaire Bride Test (#3)

The Billionaire Daddy Test (#4)

The Billionaire Matchmaker Test (#5)

The Billionaire Glitch Date (#6)

The Billionaire Perfect Date (#7)

The Billionaire Replacement Date (#8)

The Billionaire Wedding Date (#9)

Cajun Magic Mystery Series

Voodoo on the Bayou (#1)

Voodoo for Two (#2)

Deja Voodoo (#3)

Cajun Magic Mysteries Books 1-3

The Outriders

Homicide at Whiskey Gulch (#1)

Hideout at Whiskey Gulch (#2)

Held Hostage at Whiskey Gulch (#3)

Setup at Whiskey Gulch (#4)

Missing Witness at Whiskey Gulch (#5)

Cowboy Justice at Whiskey Gulch (#6)

Boys Behaving Badly Anthologies

Rogues (#1)

Blue Collar (#2)

Pirates (#3)

Stranded (#4)

First Responder (#5)

Cowboys (#6)

Silver Soldiers (#7)

Secret Identities (#8)

Made in United States
Orlando, FL
16 November 2024

53955757R00124